Ares .... **n**
witho.............

And froze.

Her hair, a soft brown, had been styled into loose, tumbling waves that fell over her shoulders and down her back. The dress was subdued and yet that didn't matter. Somehow even the fact it was minimalistic—a simple black with a halter neck and a full skirt that fell all the way to the floor—made her look elegant and regal.

"You're stunning."

Bea's lips quirked. "That sounds a lot like something someone flirting with their date might say."

"Only a fool would deny the truth."

"Flattery will get you nowhere, Mr. Lykaios."

He shook his head. "No. Tonight you will call me Ares, as you did earlier."

Her lips parted and the regret was back. Not regret that he was spending time with Bea, but that it was to be at a ball, surrounded by other people. This was a woman he would have enjoyed spending time with alone. Now, *that* would have been an actual distraction...

"And I will flatter you whenever I see fit."

Signed, Sealed...Seduced

Billion-dollar deals and breathtaking passion!

At boarding school, Clare, Bea and Amy formed an unbreakable bond. Years later, they're making waves as the owners of their own successful PR company. But having billionaires for clients means the most unexpected tasks...and *temptation*...can be thrown in their paths at a moment's notice!

Amy is sent to the Mediterranean kingdom of Vallia by the unusual request to ruin King Luca's image. What she doesn't expect is to be the center of the scandal!

Read more in
Ways to Ruin a Royal Reputation by Dani Collins

Shy Bea is left alone to handle their most important client, Ares! First job: accompany him to a Venetian ball...

Find out more in
Cinderella's Night in Venice by Clare Connelly

After escaping from criminals, Clare stows away on tycoon Dev's yacht. When he finds her, they have a convenient deal to strike!

Discover more in
The Playboy's "I Do" Deal by Tara Pammi

Clare Connelly

CINDERELLA'S NIGHT IN VENICE

Special thanks and acknowledgment are given to
Clare Connelly for her contribution to the
Signed, Sealed...Seduced miniseries.

ISBN-13: 978-1-335-40408-4

Cinderella's Night in Venice

Recycling programs
for this product may
not exist in your area.

Printed in U.S.A.

Clare Connelly was raised in small-town Australia among a family of avid readers. She spent much of her childhood up a tree, Harlequin book in hand. Clare is married to her own real-life hero, and they live in a bungalow near the sea with their two children. She is frequently found staring into space—a surefire sign she is in the world of her characters. She has a penchant for French food and ice-cold champagne, and Harlequin novels continue to be her favorite-ever books. Writing for Harlequin Presents is a long-held dream. Clare can be contacted via clareconnelly.com or on her Facebook page.

Books by Clare Connelly

Harlequin Presents

Redemption of the Untamed Italian
The Secret Kept from the King
Hired by the Impossible Greek
Their Impossible Desert Match

Secret Heirs of Billionaires

Shock Heir for the King

A Billion-Dollar Singapore Christmas

An Heir Claimed by Christmas
No Strings Christmas
(Available from Harlequin DARE)

Crazy Rich Greek Weddings

The Greek's Billion-Dollar Baby
Bride Behind the Billion-Dollar Veil

Visit the Author Profile page
at Harlequin.com for more titles.

To the indomitable spirit of the people of Italy,
and for the city of Venice.

CHAPTER ONE

'OH, MY GOD.' Bea stared at the fast-spreading blob of coffee with a look of sheer mortification on her dainty features. 'I'm so sorry. I didn't see you.'

The man—at least, he *looked* part-man, yet he was also part-warrior, all broad shoulders, lean muscle and hard-edged face—stared at her with surprise first, and then displeasure. 'Evidently.'

'Please, let me—' She cast an eye around for something—anything—she could use to mop up the man's shirt, which now bore the marks of her early evening energy boost. 'I just made it. It must be hot. Does it hurt?'

'I'll live.'

She grimaced, looking around the office, but it was past six and almost everyone had left. 'Let me just grab—' She plucked a tissue from a box on a nearby desk, lifting it to his shirt and wiping furiously, all the colour draining from her face when she realised she was only making it worse. Little white caterpillars of tissue detritus were sticking to the coffee stain, damaging the obviously expensive shirt even more.

His fingers curled around her wrist, arresting her

progress, and warmth enveloped her out of nowhere, shocking her into looking up into his face properly for the first time. At five foot ten she generally found she was almost at eye level with most men but not this guy. He stood a good few inches above her, at least six foot two, she guessed.

There was something familiar about him, though she was sure they'd never met. She'd definitely have remembered him. His face was angular and strong, like his body, a square jaw covered in dark facial hair—not a look that was cultivated or painstakingly trendy so much as a fast-growing five o'clock shadow. His lips were curved and bracketed on either side by a deep groove, like parentheses in his face, his cheekbones were prominent and his brows were thick and dark, framing his grey eyes in a way that turned the already spectacular specimens into works of art.

Her breath caught in her throat and she pulled at her hand on autopilot, a familiar instinct to deny anything approaching closeness marking her actions, her lips twisting in a silent gesture of rejection and simultaneous apology. 'Naturally the London Connection will cover the dry-cleaning fees,' she offered, her cheeks growing hot under his continued inspection.

He held up a hand in a gesture of silence.

Bea swallowed, taking a step back. 'I didn't see you.' *Quit talking, Captain Obvious*, she derided. It was a tendency she'd worked hard to curb—speaking when nervous was a girlhood habit she'd kicked long ago. Or *thought* she had.

'Where is Clare?'

'Clare?' Bea parroted with a frown, flicking a glance at her wristwatch to be sure she had the time right. Was her friend and founder of the London Connection—a woman who was as well-regarded for her business nous as she was for being notoriously disinterested in romance and relationships—dating this guy? She hadn't mentioned anything, but something *had* been different with Clare recently. Perhaps this explained it?

'Clare Roberts—about this tall, dark brown hair? Given that you work here, I imagine you've heard of her?'

Bea's eyes narrowed at his tone, which was innately condescending. It was on the tip of her tongue to tell the man that not only had she heard of Clare, but they'd gone through almost every major event in their lives, along with Amy Miller, side by side together. The three amigos, from way back.

'We had a meeting and I do not appreciate having my time wasted.'

'Oh.' She grimaced; the oversight was unprofessional and unexpected. 'She's not here.'

'She must be.' His nostrils flared as he exhaled a deep breath. 'Please go and find her.'

'Find her?' Bea felt like a parrot, but her senses were in overdrive.

'You know, walk through the office until you discover where exactly she is?' He spoke slowly, as though Bea was having difficulty comprehending what he was saying, when his English was perfect, albeit tinged with a spicy, exotic accent that was doing funny things to her pulse points.

Old feelings of inadequacy were stealing through her, making her stomach swirl with a very familiar sense of unease. She tried to banish it, forcing a tight smile to her face. 'Clare was called away on urgent business,' Bea explained, a pinprick of worry at her friend's inexplicable and urgent departure pulling at her. 'Is there anything I can help you with, Mr...?' She let her question hover in the air, allowing him time to offer a name.

His brows knitted together, and every cell in his body exuded impatience. 'You must be mistaken. This meeting has been scheduled for weeks. I flew in this afternoon for this specific purpose.'

Bea's eyes opened wide. If that was true, then they'd bungled something—badly—and that ran contrary to every instinct she possessed. 'Oh.'

'Yes,' he clipped, crossing his arms over his chest and glaring—there was really no other way to describe his expression—at her across the space. The air between them seemed to grow thick with a tension that made Bea feel as though she was continually cresting over the high point of a roller coaster. She dug the fingernails of one hand into her palm, forcing her expression to remain neutral with effort.

'As I said, something urgent came up, otherwise I know Clare wouldn't have left you in the lurch.' She waved a hand in the direction of Clare's office, the lights off, door closed. 'If you give me a moment, I can try to get in contact with her, or log into her calendar and see if—'

He scowled fiercely. 'This is completely unaccept-able.'

Bea hesitated, unprepared for this man's obvious frustration. When he was cross, like this, his accent grew thicker, more mysterious and honeyed.

'I do not have time to be messed around, nor to ac-cept excuses from some secretary or cleaner or what-ever the hell you are. I've worked with Clare a long time, but this is—'

Bea felt as though she were drowning. She'd only been with the London Connection for a few months but she knew what this company meant to her friends. Not to mention what it meant to her! This PR firm was im-portant to all of them and, whoever this man was, she didn't want to have a disgruntled client on her hands.

'Yes, very disappointing,' Bea inserted, belatedly remembering that while she was relatively new to the firm she was also the head of the legal department, having been recruited across from her senior partner role in a top tier City firm. She wasn't accustomed to being spoken to as if she were the dirt on someone's shoe. Modulating her voice to project an air of calm au-thority, she met his eyes straight on, her spine jolting at the clarity of their steel-grey pigment. They were like pewter; she wasn't sure she'd ever seen anything like it before. 'Unfortunately, standing here firing scorn and derision at me isn't going to achieve very much, is it?'

His shock was unmistakable. His eyes widened, flashing with an emotion she couldn't register, and then his jaw moved as though he was grinding his teeth to-gether.

'I am not—'

She expelled a soft breath as she cut in. 'Yes, you were, but that's okay. I understand you're disappointed. And I am truly sorry that you've flown to London from—'

He said nothing.

She waved a hand through the air. 'Wherever, only to find Clare not here.' She turned, moving towards her friend's office. 'You mentioned that you've worked with Clare for a long time, so obviously you're aware how unusual this is. I hope you're able to overlook this rare mistake.'

'I am not generally in the habit of forgiving mistakes, rare or not.'

A shiver ran down her spine at the steel in his words. She didn't doubt for a second that he meant what he said. There was an air of implacability about the man that she'd felt from the minute he'd arrived.

Bea had, at first, thought his accent was Italian, but as he spoke more, her appraisal changed. She was almost certain he was from Greece—one of her favourite places in the world. She'd spent a summer there during her degree, and had fallen in love with the sun, the water, the history and, most of all, the anonymity. When she travelled abroad, no one knew Bea as Beatrice Jones, daughter of Rock Legend Ronnie Jones and Supermodel Alice Jones.

'Then I hope you'll make an exception just this once,' she implored as she flicked Clare's screen to life, typing in her friend's password quickly. 'Please, have a seat.'

He glowered at her without speaking.

A dislike for this rude, arrogant man was forming in her gut. She knew she couldn't treat any client of the firm's with disrespect but the way he was acting was truly unforgivable! So Clare had made an unusual mistake. It obviously wasn't ideal, but nor was it the end of the world.

'Now, let's see if Clare's left any notes here,' Bea murmured, reaching for a pen and tapping it on the edge of the desk.

'Should you be doing this?'

She frowned, looking up at him.

'I cannot imagine Clare would want just anyone accessing her files. There'll be sensitive information in there, including financial documents.' Suspicion crept into his voice. 'What exactly is your role within the company?'

She double-clicked into Clare's calendar as she prepared to answer him but, before she could speak, all the breath whooshed out of her lungs. His name hovered on the screen before Bea, in black and white pixels.

Ares Lykaios.

AKA the firm's most important, gazillionaire, global tycoon client. This man had a finger in just about every corporate pie imaginable. From transport and logistics to airlines to textiles and telecommunications, as well as casinos and hotels, Ares Lykaios had been given the nickname 'Gold Fingers' at some point because, as the press liked to say, everything he touched had a habit of turning to gold.

He was also a man both Clare and Amy had pulled Bea aside to warn her about.

'He's intelligent, demanding, ruthless and loaded. Deep down he's a good enough guy, probably, but he expects top level service—and doesn't suffer fools gladly.'

'Should your path ever cross his, which it likely won't because he only deals with Clare, do whatever you can to keep him happy—we can't afford to lose his business.'

Bea gulped, her eyes straying to the man's stained shirt with renewed panic.

'Mr Lykaios.' Her voice was strangled in her throat, unwanted nerves robbing her of any confidence. She shook her head, forcing herself to project professional authority. She stood, wiping her palms surreptitiously down the sides of her pencil skirt. 'I'm Beatrice Jones, head of legal here at the London Connection. Allow me to apologise once more—'

'No more apologies.' His eyes, grey like the strongest steel, seemed to lance her. 'I am not in the mood.'

'Then why don't you allow me to organise you a drink—perhaps something to eat?—while I familiarise myself with your file. I don't have Clare's or Amy's experience, of course, but I'm sure I'll be able to—'

'I have absolutely no desire to be palmed off with someone who, by her own admission, doesn't have the skill set required to manage my interests.'

Bea's jaw dropped. 'Mr Lykaios—' her voice shook a little with indignation '—please don't misunderstand the situation. While Clare isn't physically here right now, she's as involved in the business as always. As is Amy. You're in very good hands, I assure you.'

'Really? Because it certainly doesn't feel that way.'

He pushed his fingers through his hair, which was thick and dark, cropped to the nape of his neck. The action conveyed obvious irritation. Bea's eyes, though, were drawn to his torso; she couldn't help noticing the way his expensive business shirt pulled across his obviously taut abdomen, the spilled coffee highlighting the definition of his pectoral muscles.

For as long as she'd known them, Amy and Clare had pushed Bea, telling her she needed to be more assertive. To tell her parents how she felt. To speak up about the hurt rendered in her childhood, and to stand up to the partners who'd pushed their workload onto Bea's desk, all the while claiming the hours for themselves. Her best friends had pushed her to speak up about *anything*, and Bea always smiled and nodded, knowing their words were kindly meant—and definitely not something she would ever act on. Yet anger rushed through her suddenly, and for one ghastly moment she was terrified of unleashing it all on this man.

With no Clare and no Amy in the office—and Bea new enough to still be grappling with clients and staff— she'd had a demanding enough day already. Straightening her spine, she gestured once more to the seat across from her. 'Please, take a seat. Tell me what you need.'

'What I need is for my usual PR manager to discuss the launch of a seven-billion-dollar operation in Mexico and Brazil. Do you feel you can discuss the nuances of that, Miss…?'

'Jones,' Beatrice supplied and, despite the tension humming between them, she was glad he hadn't heard of her. Glad for some of that Greek anonymity to be here in this room.

'Well, Miss Jones—'

'Please, call me Bea,' she suggested, aware that she needed to break down his barriers—and quickly—if she was going to have any hope of defusing this situation.

Bea. The name was short and brief, jarring and unpleasant. He dismissed it, wondering why she had chosen to use this moniker instead of her actual name. In the back of his mind, Ares knew he was being a first-rate bastard. He could see the pretty young woman was close to snapping point and it was an excellent indication of the kind of day—scratch that, *month*—he'd been having that he didn't care.

But 'Bea' had raised an excellent point. He'd come to Clare Roberts about three months after she'd opened the firm a couple of years ago, and he'd never once wavered in his choice to support her fledgling PR company. He'd witnessed her go from strength to strength and had always admired the work she'd done for him. Surely she'd earned a little leeway from him?

Yes, she had, undoubtedly, but at the moment all of Ares's leeway was in use.

His phone began to buzz in his top pocket.

'Now, just give me a moment, and I'll see if Clare's made any—'

He held up a hand to silence her, reaching for his phone and swiping it to answer. He understood the look of displeasure that crossed Bea's face at his obviously rude gesture.

Another tick in the 'bastard' column for him.

'Lykaios,' he barked into the receiver.

'It's Cassandra.'

He closed his eyes, his stomach immediately sinking. The fact that the nanny he'd hired for his infant niece was calling yet again was definitely *not* a good sign. The last time it had been to beg off the assignment, telling him she wasn't equipped to 'cope' with the child. Danica was only five months old! How hard could it be?

'Go ahead.'

'I gave it another shot, I did, but honestly, she's impossible.'

He tossed his head back, staring up at the ceiling as he rubbed his fingers across his neck. 'Isn't that what you're supposed to be trained to deal with?'

'I'm a nanny, not a magician.'

He could have laughed if he wasn't already at breaking point. 'Your résumé and references are excellent,' he reminded Cassandra.

'Yes, I know. But I don't generally work with infants, and definitely not infants like Danica. She needs—'

'Whatever she needs, she can have. But right now, I need you.' He compressed his lips, the sense of flailing out of control horrifying him, so he stood taller, straighter, staring directly ahead at the wall across the room. 'Double the agreed salary, Cassandra. Just do your damned job.' He hung up before she could answer, confident the exorbitant pay he was offering would be too tempting to turn down.

It wasn't Bea's fault, but when he turned back to her, his mood had dipped into oblivion.

'You are telling me Clare thinks so little of my business she has disappeared into thin air and left only *you* to help?'

The insult hit its mark. He almost regretted the words. It was beneath him to treat anyone like this. But the look of fire that stoked in the depths of her eyes was fascinating and somehow compelling. He moved closer, bracing his palms on the back of the leather chair she kept trying to wave him into.

'I'm not sure what your implication is,' she murmured, her cultured English accent irking him far more than it should.

'Aren't you?' he drawled, a mocking smile curving his lips. He wasn't amused though. He was frustrated and angry, just as he'd been since his younger brother had checked himself into rehab—thank God—after too many benders to ignore, stranding the infant Danica with Ares, a man completely unsuited to being responsible for anyone, let alone a baby. All his life he'd been taking care of others, and failing them at the same time. His mother. His brother. And now his niece. Why wouldn't they see that Ares was a loner—not meant to be depended on by anyone?

He dug his fingers into the back of the chair until the flesh beneath his nails turned white.

'Look, Mr Lykaios, I appreciate how you must be feeling. This is so unlike the London Connection. You mentioned you'd flown into London for the meeting. Will you still be here tomorrow?'

'I wasn't planning to be.'

Her delicate jaw moved as she bit back whatever it

was she'd been about to say. Goading her was giving him the most pleasure he'd felt in weeks. Irrational and stupid, he knew he shouldn't bother, yet sparking off this woman offered a kind of tension release.

'If you could perhaps see your way to changing your plans, I can spend tonight familiarising myself with the campaign proposal and meet with you again in the morning.'

'And can you promise you'll offer me exactly the same level of service and expertise Clare ordinarily would?'

'Well, given that I'm head of the legal department and I'm more comfortable wading through hundreds of pages of technical contracts than analysing public relations, I can't promise *exactly* the same level of expertise, but I think you'll find me sufficiently well-informed.'

They stared at each other across the desk; it was impossible to say who was more surprised. Ares for having succeeded in stirring her into the outburst, or Bea for having given in to the sarcastic flood of words.

She clamped a hand to her lips, shaking her head. 'I'm sorry; that was rude.'

'Yes, it was,' he agreed, brushing aside her words and still taking a perverse pleasure in making her sweat. 'I have already told you though: I'm not interested in apologies.'

Her eyes swept shut, her dark lashes forming two perfect crescent fan shapes against her creamy cheeks.

'As for your offer—' he loaded the word with as much condemnation as he could, in no mood to be messed around after everything else he'd been through '—I'll take it into consideration.'

She frowned. 'What exactly does that mean?'

'That I'll see how I feel in the morning. Do your homework, Miss Johns. If I'm here, I'll expect you to be prepared.'

She hadn't even corrected him on her surname! 'It's Jones,' she'd intended to snap, but the words had died on the tip of her tongue, as they often did when confronted with people who treated her as he had just done. Instead, she'd watched him stalk away through the offices, his pace long and feral, anger emanating off him in waves.

She sank into her chair with a worried expression, staring at Clare's computer with wariness. She was *not* a public relations expert and she wasn't interested in becoming one, but she would protect this business with every fibre of her being. And that meant fixing this monumental mess-up, or risk losing their biggest client.

Not on her watch. It would be a long night, but that was nothing new to Bea. For the sake of the company, she'd do whatever it took. Even suffer through another meeting with that arrogant bastard of a man.

CHAPTER TWO

ADDICTION WAS A beast of a thing. While Ares's younger brother had struggled with it most of his life, following in the footsteps of their drug-addicted mother, Ares had never found that this demon resided within him. It was one reason he could pour himself a measure of Scotch some time before midnight, aware that one measure would bring him the sense of mental tranquillity he craved—but that one small measure would be sufficient. Unlike Matthaios, Ares had never drunk to excess, nor had he indulged in a penchant for drugs. Being in control was essential for him, and he sought that feeling whenever and however he could.

Drinking to excess or taking mind-altering substances was anathema to him. Perhaps that explained why he'd let his brother down so badly. If he'd shared the same proclivities as Matthaios, maybe Ares would have been better placed to help him. He might have seen the path ahead sooner, foreshadowing Matthaios's unravelling after Ingrid's untimely death. The loss of Matthaios's beloved wife in childbirth, coupled with the burden of a screaming newborn, had obviously been too much for a man who'd struggled with addictive impulses all his life.

Ares's grip tightened around the Scotch glass, his eyes chasing the lights of London's renowned skyline. It was a view he drew little comfort from—he far preferred the outlook from his home on Porto Heli. Yet tonight he stared across the ancient city with a feeling that this was the only place he wanted to be in the world.

Or was it that his home was the *last* place he wanted to be? With the screaming, unsettled, demanding infant in residence, and a nanny looking to break the contract he'd had her sign before undertaking the assignment, Porto Heli had temporarily lost its charms. Every time he looked into little Danica's eyes he felt a suffocating sense of failure.

The baby deserved better than him. Just as Matthaios had deserved better than to be raised by Ares, just as he should have been able to save their mother and hadn't. It was history repeating itself over and over and Ares had no doubt he was out of his depth. Which was why he'd hired the best nanny he could find, a woman who came highly recommended by several sources. It was something he would never have dreamed of affording as a teenager. He and Matt had been on their own: poor, starving, alone, and Ares had had to do the best he could—and live with the fact that it had never been quite enough. But for Danica it was different. He could provide her with a nanny for as long as necessary, making sure she would always have what she needed.

Except that Cassandra, the nanny, had been threatening to quit for over a week.

If he wasn't in Greece, perhaps human decency would force her hand. Perhaps she'd decide the right thing to do was stay. Perhaps she'd bond with the baby and decide she couldn't leave her. And perhaps a drift of pigs would fly past his window right now.

He threw back the rest of the Scotch, cradling the empty glass in the palm of his hand.

The meeting this evening had been the last straw. Clare Roberts from the London Connection was someone he saw a few times a year and corresponded with marginally more frequently. She was incredibly organised, professional and detail-oriented and he'd been needing someone like that today. He'd wanted to walk in there and know that everything was in order in at least one aspect of his life.

Instead he'd got *Bea*. Her name bothered him less now than it had earlier. In fact, when he heard it in his mind, he saw her cupid's bow lips framing the word and almost felt the soft rush of her breath across his cheek.

Something like shame gripped him as he recalled their interaction, everything he'd said to her slamming into him now, so he felt as though he'd taken out the hell his life had turned into on the first person he'd found he could blame for something. Yes, he'd used her to unleash his tension simply because he'd reached his limits, and that had been inexcusable.

Right before he fell asleep, Ares resolved to fix that—he'd been unreasonable, but he could undo whatever damage his tirade had caused. Tomorrow was a new day; perhaps things would look better in the morning.

* * *

'Mr Lykaios, please, take a seat.' Any hopes Bea had held that the arrogant billionaire might have become less good-looking overnight evaporated into thin air when he strode into the office a little after midday. Wearing a dark grey suit with a crisp white shirt flicked open at the neck to reveal the strong column of his neck, he was preposterously hot. Seriously, was it necessary for him to have *that* face, and *that* body? Wouldn't one or the other have sufficed? Strong features, chiselled jaw, eyes you could drown in, and a body that looked as though he could run marathons before breakfast. Bea's physical reaction was inevitable. Her mouth went dry and her stomach swooped, but she told herself the latter was owing to nerves.

After the disastrous 'meeting' the evening before, she'd spent most of the night reading every single thing she could on the man and his business, as well as swotting up on the current public relations undertakings the firm was making on his behalf. And that was no mean feat. He was a dynamo in the corporate world, with interests all over the globe. The London Connection was currently overseeing ten specific campaigns, as well as doing ad hoc PR work as the need arose. There were four staff members dedicated to him full-time, with Clare managing their work diligently, as—according to the file on Ares Lykaios, he preferred to have only one contact rather than needing to get to know 'new people'.

Strike one, she was out.

As with the evening before, he ignored the chair, striding towards Bea instead, his pewter-grey eyes latched onto hers in a way that made her tummy flip and flop.

'Miss Jones.' He nodded in greeting and her tummy stopped flipping and started feeling as though it were under assault from a kaleidoscope of over-excited butterflies. He held out a hand and she slid hers into it on autopilot, but the second his fingers curled around hers Bea's eyes flew wide, locking on Ares's in shock. Sparks of electricity seemed to be exploding through her, heat travelling from the pads of his fingers to the centre of her being. Her breath was burning in her lungs and heat stole across her cheeks. She dragged her eyes away; it did little to alleviate her physical awareness of the man. Great, that was all she needed: to be *attracted* to this mega-client.

Bea had a minuscule degree of experience with men, and had always been glad she was far too plain and dull to attract anyone's attention. That wasn't strictly true—she'd been asked out on dates before, but the very idea of a relationship had made Bea feel as if her skin was being scrubbed with acid and she'd always backed off. Meaning she'd never had first-date tingles or a blush of attraction when a man she liked looked into her eyes as though he might find the meaning of life in their depths.

Whoa. Hold on. She didn't *like* Ares Lykaios. He was a client first and foremost, and her ingrained professionalism and diligence prohibited her from thinking about him on any other level. But even if she were inclined to fantasise—which she definitely, truly wasn't—how was she forgetting the way he'd treated her the night before? She'd grown up with enough spoiled, entitled, arrogant people in her orbit to know that these were her least favourite qualities.

Their hands were still joined. She pulled away jerkily, wiping her palm on the side of her trousers. That did nothing at all to stop the tingling in her fingertips.

'I had some refreshments ordered in,' she offered politely, pleased when her voice emerged cool and crisp. She sounded far more in control than she felt. 'Pastries, fruit, sandwiches. Please, help yourself.'

His dark head dipped in silent acknowledgement, but he didn't reach for any food. Instead, she watched as he lifted the sterling silver coffee pot and poured a measure into a mug. His focus was on what he was doing, which meant she could watch him—unguarded for a moment. As he poured the coffee, his sleeve shifted a fraction higher, revealing the flicking tail of a tattoo—cursive script, perhaps?—running up his wrist. Curiosity sparked in her belly; she tamped down on it post-haste. This wasn't the time to be wondering about his tattoo, or his body.

Except…she found it almost impossible to stop.

He was tanned, as though he spent a lot of time outdoors. Given that it was only April, it suggested he lived in a warmer climate than London, which was just starting to see some clear blue sky and warmth thaw the ground. Bea had always hated the cold. It reminded her of long nights at boarding school when the blankets had never felt quite warm enough. Or perhaps it was more the ice in her heart, an ice that repeated rejections—first by her biological parents and then her adoptive ones—had locked in place.

His lashes were long and thick, the kind supermodels would kill for. As Bea knew first-hand—she'd witnessed her mother's attempts at enhancement for long enough to understand what went into procuring such thick and radiant eye furnishings.

Unexpectedly, he jerked his gaze to her face and heat spread through her. Guilt too, at having been caught staring. She looked down at the tabletop in a knee-jerk response.

'Coffee for you?'

She nodded quickly, taking up the seat at the head of the table. 'Thanks. I've already had three cups this morning but if it weren't for coffee I have no idea how I'd get by. I should have credited my law degree to the stuff.' *Stop. Talking. For the love of God.*

He was the opposite to her. Silent and brooding, pouring the coffee with his long fingers holding the mug mid-air, replacing the pot then striding to her side of the table. Close enough for Bea to inhale his intoxicatingly masculine fragrance. Her gut kicked. What the hell was happening? She'd made an art form out of ignoring the opposite sex. Why was she suddenly obsessed with details like his tantalising cologne and curly eyelashes?

To her chagrin, Ares Lykaios, all six feet plus of him, folded himself into the seat directly to her right, so close that if she hadn't moved quickly their legs would have become entangled beneath the table. Her pulse was in frantic overdrive at the very idea! She wrapped her hands around her coffee cup and stared at the swirling steam rather than look at him again.

'Try not to spill it on me this time.' The words were serious but she felt an undercurrent of amusement in their throaty depths. It unsettled her completely.

'Shall we begin?' She didn't sound remotely cool now. Her words were still crisp, but closer to being whispered, as though she were afraid of him.

Get a bloody grip, Bea!

She conjured an image of Clare on one side of her and Amy the other, their smiling, encouraging faces providing much-needed strength. But there was also the spectre of fear—what would happen if she bungled this and lost the firm's most important client? Clare had ploughed all her inheritance money into this place, and it had finally given her a sense of purpose and safety. Bea could never let anything happen to the London Connection on her watch.

'Soon.' The word dropped between them, shaking Bea out of her thoughts. She frowned, looking at him.

He was studying her now with the same intense curiosity she'd focused on him earlier. Bea *hated* to be looked at and actively did everything she could to discourage that kind of attention, but what could she do now? Tell him to stop? Tell him she didn't like it? When the truth was, a strange kind of warmth was bubbling through her blood and her lips were parted on a husky breath of surrender.

Why was he looking at her, though? Bea was under no false illusions regarding her looks. Her adoptive mother was a supermodel and her younger twin sisters had inherited their mother's looks, all slender and fine-boned, blonde and blue-eyed, with skin as translucent as milk and honey. She'd known from a very young age she didn't compare and, even if she hadn't understood that, the articles the press had run through her teenage years—when pimples and puppy fat had attached to Bea with gusto—had left her in little doubt as to her physical merits, or lack thereof. After suffering comparisons to her mother at the same age, and then the twins, Bea had eventually developed a thick skin, yet only after years of painful arrows had already hit their mark.

But who cared about that stuff anyway? she reminded herself staunchly. She'd never wanted to be known for her looks—how vapid and dull! That was just genetic lottery. Far better to build a reputation based on hard work and effort. Tilting her chin, it was on the tip of her tongue to say something to bring their meeting back on track, except he was staring at her mouth now, and logical thoughts were suddenly impossible. Self-conscious, she bit down on the edge of her lip, wiggling it from side to side. She stopped when she saw the way his forehead creased, his thick brows drawn together speculatively.

'I—' She spoke because the silence was like the beating of a drum, resonating in the air around them and deep within her, demanding action—inciting a physical response which was new to her. Her pulse was hammering in the same way, rhythmic and urgent, low and slow, echoing throughout her whole body.

But her attempt at starting a sentence seemed to rouse him. He shifted, reaching for his coffee cup, taking a sip before returning his eyes to hers. Sparks flew through her.

'I came to apologise.'

It was the very last thing she'd expected him to say.

'What?' She shook her head from side to side, a be-mused expression on her features. 'I mean, I'm sorry?'

His lips twisted. 'You stole my line.'

Her smile was instinctive. 'But—what for?'

'You don't think my behaviour last night warrants an apology?'

She looked down at the gleaming conference table, un-sure how to answer. She wasn't going to tell Mr Millions-of-Pounds-in-Revenue that he'd been incredibly rude. Besides, he evidently knew that already.

'It's fine, honestly.'

'It is *not* fine. The fact Clare missed our meeting was not your fault. I shouldn't have taken my displea-sure out on you.'

Her pulse began to race for another reason now. His apology was limited specifically to her. The company wasn't out of the woods yet. Bea still had work to do.

'I'm a senior team member of the London Connec-tion,' she said firmly. 'I should have known you were expecting to meet with Clare, and I should have been prepared. It was an oversight none of us has ever made before. It's I who should apologise.'

His eyes remained glued to hers as he took another mouthful of coffee, so a shiver ran down her spine. Not a cold shiver, though. More like that delightful sensa-tion one experienced when sinking into a warm, fra-granced bath on a cool night. Pleasure radiated through her. She jerked her eyes away, forcibly angling her head a little so there was no risk of meeting his eyes again.

'Then we were both at fault,' he agreed. 'But to different degrees.'

Something like amusement snaked through her at his determination to take the blame for their catastrophic meeting the evening before. 'You don't strike me as a man who apologises often, and yet you do it well.'

'I may have an ulterior motive to earning your forgiveness.'

'Oh?'

'There's an event tonight, and I need a date to accompany me.'

Bea's pulse ramped up. She quickly looked down at the iPad on the tabletop, trying to remember every detail from the files she'd read overnight. 'I—can't remember seeing that,' she admitted belatedly, curving her hands around her own coffee cup to stop them from shaking visibly. 'Is that something we usually arrange for you, Mr Lykaios?'

His eyes widened and then he tipped his head back on a laugh that reverberated around the room, rich in timbre and heavy in amusement. She sipped her coffee, simply for the comfort its familiar taste would bring.

'I am asking *you* on a date, Bea, not to act as an escort service.'

Now it was Bea's turn to be surprised. 'Just to be your escort then?'

The humour was gone. Something far more troubling flared in the depths of his eyes. Despite zero practical experience with men she'd still watched enough movies to recognise sensual appraisal. Her knees felt as though they'd been pumped full of water and she was grateful she was sitting or she might have fallen down.

'The event is high-profile and will be covered extensively in the press. I'd prefer not to arrive alone. Think of it as a PR service.'

Every fibre in her body screamed at her to say no. All the buzz words she'd learned to fear and hate were in that sentence. Press. PR. Event. High-profile. She stared at her coffee, sure her face must look whiter than a sheet of paper. 'Mr Lykaios, I'm afraid that's not possible.'

'You're involved with someone?'

Her heart thumped against her ribcage. 'No,' she said before she could think better of it, denying herself a simple explanation for her demurral. 'Not exactly.'

'What does "not exactly" mean?'

'I'm not seeing anyone,' she grumbled, biting down on her lip once more.

'Even if you were, it wouldn't matter,' he said after a pause. 'This isn't a romantic invitation, Bea. It's just work. A small way you can make up for the inconvenience of last night.'

His words were a form of torture. On the one hand reassuring, because she didn't *want* to go on an actual date with someone like him—or anyone. But the fact that he was taking such great pains to tell her this wasn't romantic speared her with unmistakable disappointment.

'Or,' she murmured thoughtfully, 'I can go through the information I ascertained about your PR concerns, and you can go through your no doubt extensive Rolodex of past dates and choose someone else to accompany you.'

Oh, my God. She lifted a hand to her lips again, her eyes drowning in his as the whip of her words cracked through the room. 'I'm sorry. Again,' she mumbled, shaking her head.

'I meant what I said last night. I do not have any interest in apologies.'

The hypocrisy of that stung. '*You* came here to apologise.'

'I was in the wrong.'

'I thought we just agreed I was too.'

He dipped his head. 'I'm asking you to show me you're sorry. That's far more valuable to me than empty words.'

'By going to some event with you?'

'Precisely.'

'But why?'

'I've already answered that.'

'Because you don't want to arrive alone?'

His eyes narrowed. 'In part, yes.'

'Then, as I said, perhaps you could consider—'

'Inviting someone else?' He brushed that suggestion aside. 'I'm asking you.'

'I don't understand why.'

'Because it's tonight, and you're here.'

'I'm here?'

'Yes. Available and in my debt.'

Her lips parted. 'I wouldn't exactly say that.'

His teeth were bared in an approximation of a grin. 'Wouldn't you?'

Damn him. He knew what he was worth to this business, and he knew she'd do just about anything to keep him happy.

And he was right. She sensed the jeopardy they were in, and no way would she do anything to worsen it. If going to some event with this man was the price she had to pay to keep him happy then she'd do it. She'd do it for Clare and she'd do it for Amy, even though it was the last thing she personally wanted!

'I'd have conditions,' she mused.

'I'm all ears.'

He definitely wasn't all ears. He was all hot, handsome face and Greek god body. That was a huge part of her problem. She'd never found a man it was harder to ignore.

'This isn't romantic in any way. Under no circumstances will there be any touching, kissing or flirting.'

'Agreed.' Why then did his droll smile feel exactly like flirtation? Inwardly, she groaned.

'It's only for one night. After which you'll drop me home and that's the end of it.'

'Isn't that covered by rule number one?'

'I'm a lawyer; what can I say? Specificity is my stock in trade.'

'Fine,' he agreed, his voice warm with amusement. 'I won't look to seduce you on a technicality then.'

Fire burst through her. She could no longer sit at the table, so close to him. Instead, she stood, pacing to the windows that overlooked the bustling streets of London. She wore a slightly oversized trouser suit but the sunlight streaming in through the window highlighted her slender silhouette. She was unaware of the way Ares's eyes lingered on her body, appreciating her shape—her breasts, the curve of her hips—or she would have sprinted from the natural light as though a tiger was on her tail.

'And you'll forget about yesterday completely,' she added.

She wasn't looking at him, and Ares didn't speak for a while. 'I can't do that.'

She gaped, turning to face him. 'It was a mistake, Ares,' she pleaded, forgetting momentarily to address him more formally, then wishing she hadn't when that same look of sensual appraisal appeared in his eyes. She was drowning, and there was no lifeline within reach.

'Not your mistake, though.'

'Yes, my mistake,' she rushed to correct him. 'I was here, and I should have—'

He stood abruptly, a warning in his gaze now as he strode towards her, fast and intent. 'I will not forget yesterday but I will forgive it, so long as you agree to accompany me this evening. Do we have a deal?'

Her heart shifted in her chest. He stood right in front of her, so close that if a gust of wind blew her forward by a matter of an inch or so they'd be touching. She took a stilted step back, an awkward gesture that didn't escape his notice, if his slightly mocking look was anything to go by.

'Not quite.'

'More details?'

Her lips twisted in wry agreement. 'Always. I don't need you to forgive me or forget yesterday, but I do need you to promise to give the London Connection another chance. Allow me to have this meeting with you now, seeing as I spent all night preparing for it. Or to call in one of my colleagues, who actually does most of the grunt work on your case and would be far better versed and able to answer your—'

He pressed a finger to her mouth and every cell in her body began to tremble. Her lips were like lava, her face bursting with heat.

'No.'

Her stomach dropped but Bea was unable to feel as much disappointment as she should have. Instead, her body was intent on making her aware of just how nice it was to be touched by him.

'I can wait until Clare returns.'

'I don't know how long she's away for, but I'm sure she can do a virtual meeting at the earliest convenience.'

'I will arrange this.'

Bea's heart thundered.

'I have some conditions of my own.'

His finger lingered on her lips. She was glad; already she feared its removal, her own rules be damned.

'Yes?'

'This is a ball. You will need to dress appropriately.'

More heat stole through Bea. A ball was so far down on her list of favourite ways to spend time, she practically classified it as a torture technique. She gritted her teeth. For the good of the company and all that. 'Fine.'

His finger drifted slowly across her lips, moving sideways, travelling down to her chin and lifting it slightly.

'I have drawn a line in the sand under yesterday. We do not need to discuss it again. Come tonight, be a charming date on my arm and I can promise you there will be no ramifications for the unprofessional mishap.'

She went hot and cold all at once. Bea had no doubt he knew exactly what he was doing—incentivising her cooperation with the most lightly delivered threat. But why would he care so much about having her accompany him?

His fingers stayed on her chin, the touch light, so she wanted more, and that very idea had her lips parting. 'You're already breaking rule one.'

Was it her imagination, or did Ares move closer? 'You think this is flirting?' he asked huskily.

Her heart skipped a beat. She nodded, dislodging his finger and telling herself she was glad.

He frowned. 'You're wrong. This is business, and it's best you don't forget it.'

CHAPTER THREE

As HIS CAR pulled up outside the London Connection offices, Ares wondered for the tenth time that day why he'd insisted on doing this. He'd initially gone to Bea's office intending to apologise and draw a line in the sand, leaving the matter behind him. Overnight, his temper had simmered down and he could clearly understand why he'd overreacted. Since his brother's spectacular breakdown and admission to rehab, and Danica's entry into his life, Ares had felt as though he were lurching from one disaster to another.

Clare forgetting their meeting had been the last straw and he'd taken that out on her hapless business partner.

An apology had been called for, but once he'd made it that should have been the end of it.

But the way she'd looked at him had stirred something inside him, a curiosity he couldn't quell, and Ares was determined to get the answers he craved.

He stepped out of the car, then was striding towards her office with a confident gait, pushing the door inwards and hailing the lift. The doors opened immediately; he stepped inside, watching as the buttons indicating each level glowed as he passed. When the doors pinged open to the London Connection, he acknowledged he was actually looking forward to tonight.

It was unexpected but, given it was the first time in a month he'd felt anything other than a slight sense of panic, he wasn't going to question the emotion. Ares Lykaios had used to feel like this before. Before Matt. Before Danica. He liked women, he liked spending time with them, and for the first time in a long time he felt a rush of pleasure at the prospect of a night spent with a woman who was intelligent and interesting. There was nothing more complex than that behind this evening. He was scratching an itch, giving himself a reprieve, distracting himself from the dumpster fire of his life for a few hours.

It was just after five and the office was still a hive of activity. He announced himself at Reception and was directed to Bea's office. He strode towards it, pausing to read her name on the door: Beatrice Jones. Beatrice suited her better. He knocked twice then pushed in without waiting.

And froze.

She was looking out of the window, her expression—even in profile—taut, but he spared her face only the briefest of glances. Instead, his eyes roamed her body, cataloguing the effort she'd gone to—and the effect it had on him. Her hair, a soft brown, had been styled into loose, tumbling waves that fell over her shoulders and down her back. The dress was subdued and yet that didn't matter. Somehow even the fact it was minimalistic—a simple black with a halter neck and a full skirt that fell all the way to the floor—made her look elegant and regal. When she turned to face him her expression was troubled, but she smiled as he strode towards her and any doubts about why he'd committed to this course of action fled.

'You're stunning.'

Her lips quirked. 'That sounds a lot like something someone flirting with their date might say.'

'Only a fool would deny the truth.'

'Flattery will get you nowhere, Mr Lykaios.'

He shook his head. 'No. Tonight you will call me Ares, as you did earlier.'

Her lips parted and the regret was back. Not regret that he was spending time with Bea, but that it was to be at a ball, surrounded by other people. This was a woman he would have enjoyed spending time with—alone. Now *that* would have been an actual distraction...

'And I will flatter you whenever I see fit.'

Her eyes darted to his and then looked away again, as though she were actually panicked by the very idea. More questions.

She paused at the reception desk and Ares was aware of the eyes that were trained on them—curious staff members unused to seeing a senior member of the team dressed like this. Her cheeks grew pink at the obvious attention. 'I'll have my phone for anything urgent. Please call if you need me.'

The receptionist grinned, gesturing to the lift. 'We'll be fine, Bea. Have fun.'

'So what is this event, exactly?'

'It's to mark the opening of a children's hospital. My foundation was involved in the funding.'

'Ah.' She nodded, mollified by that, as it made it all

the more obvious that this was, in fact, a work commitment. 'I read about your foundation last night. You do a lot of work with children's charities.'

'Yes.'

'I didn't realise you were involved in any in the UK though.'

'Our foundation has many partners. Often our work is indirect.'

'Silent philanthropy?'

'Attention isn't exactly the point. I do not support charitable acts because I'm looking for praise.'

'Don't you?'

The grey of his eyes turned stormy like the ocean. 'That's a rather cynical viewpoint to have.'

She laughed, unexpectedly caught off guard by that. 'You're right, it is.' How could she feel otherwise, though, given the way her adopted status had been brandished by her adoptive mother only when it suited her purposes? If she ever needed the world to see her as a Mother Teresa figure, out would come Bea, some photoshoot or other arranged to convince the world of the Jones family's altruism.

She looked towards the car window, her mood slightly dampened by the bitter reflection. 'You didn't say where we're going tonight.'

'No,' he agreed laconically. 'You're new to the London Connection?'

His change of subject was swift and she frowned, but reminded herself that he was the client and she couldn't afford to offend him again. It had nothing to do with what *she* wanted—if she had her way she'd be home bingeing Netflix, definitely not on the way to some swanky affair with this Greek god brought to life.

Before she could respond to his question, he reached for the skirt that covered her knees, lifting it a little.

Surprise had her dropping her eyes, and then, as she followed his gaze, wincing. He'd noticed her shoes. Red high-tops with their trademark white star on the sides, a little scuffed at the toe. Coupled with the sheer black stockings she wore, she was well aware they looked ridiculous.

'In case you need to run away from me?' he pondered, his smile the last word in sexy.

It was the kind of smile designed to melt ice, but Bea's frozen heart was unlike anything Ares had ever known. She offered a cool smile in return. 'Oh, absolutely. A girl never knows when she might have to break a world record.'

'Usain Bolt, eat your heart out?'

'You better believe it.'

'Seriously, though. Did you leave your shoes at home? We can stop and get them if you would like?'

Bea didn't want to admit that she'd chosen to wear these shoes out of habit—that at five foot ten she always wore flats to avoid looking like a giraffe.

'Nobody will see them beneath the dress. I'll be fine.' She just managed to avoid adding 'Won't I?'

But when she looked at him he was scrutinising her thoughtfully. She uncrossed her legs and rearranged her skirt so the hem covered her shoes.

'You were telling me about your job at the London Connection.'

'No, you were asking,' she reminded him, relieved the conversation had returned to something less personal than her choice of footwear.

He waited, watchful in that unnerving way of his.

'It was a few months ago,' she relented. 'Though Clare's been asking me to join for years.'

'You've known her a long time?'

Bea's expression assumed a nostalgic air as she thought back to her teenage years. 'The three of us went to school together. They're my best friends.'

'You're very different to Clare and Amy.'

She was, but his perceptiveness surprised her. 'In what way?'

'Many ways,' he said, the answer frustrating for its lack of clarity. The car turned towards the river. She couldn't think of any hotels here, but it had been a while since she'd ventured this way. Perhaps they were going to a converted warehouse?

'Is being similar to friends a prerequisite to friendship?'

He put his arm up along the back of her seat, his fingers dangling tantalisingly close to her shoulder. 'I couldn't say. It apparently works for you.'

That drew her interest. 'You don't have friends?'

He frowned. 'I didn't say that.'

'You kind of did.'

It was his turn to laugh. 'You're reading between the lines.'

'Do you mind?'

As the car slowed to go over a speed hump, his fingers briefly fell to her shoulder. An accident of transit, nothing intentional about it. The reason didn't matter though; the spark of electricity was the same regardless. She gasped and quickly turned her face away, looking beyond the window.

It was then that she realised they had driven through the gates of City Airport.

She turned back to face him, a question in her eyes. 'There's a ball at the airport?'

'No.'

'Then why…?' Comprehension was a blinding light. 'We're flying somewhere.'

'To the ball.'

'But…you didn't say…'

'I thought you were good at reading between the lines?'

She pouted her lips. 'Yes, you're right.' She clicked her fingers in the air. 'I should have miraculously intuited that when you invited me to a ball you meant for us to fly there. Where, exactly?'

'Venice.'

'Venice?' She stared at him, aghast. 'I don't have a passport.'

'I had your assistant arrange it.'

'You—what? When?'

'When I left this morning.'

'My assistant just handed over my passport?'

'You have a problem with that?'

'Well, gee, let me think about that a moment,' she said, tapping a finger to the side of her lip. 'You're a man I'd never clapped eyes on until yesterday and now you have in your possession a document that's of reasonably significant personal importance. You *could* say I find that a little invasive, yes.'

He dropped his hand from the back of the seat, inadvertently brushing her arm as he moved, lifting a familiar burgundy document from his pocket. 'Now you have it in *your* possession. It was no conspiracy to kidnap you, Beatrice, simply a means to an end.'

Clutching the passport in her hand, she stared down at it. No longer bothered by the fact he'd managed to convince her assistant to commandeer a document of such personal importance from her top drawer, she was knocked off-kilter by his use of her full name. Nobody called her Beatrice any more. She'd been Bea for as long as she could remember. As girls, they'd formed a club: ABC—Amy, Bea, Clare, and the 'Bea' had stuck. But her full name on his lips momentarily shoved the air from her lungs.

'Why didn't you just tell me?'

He lifted his shoulders. 'I thought you might say no.'

It was an important clue as to how he operated. This was a man who would do what he needed to achieve whatever he wanted. He'd chosen to invite her to this event, and so he'd done what he deemed necessary to have her there.

'Your business is too important to our company, remember?' She was grateful for the opportunity to remind them both of the reason she'd agreed to this. It had nothing to do with the fact she found him attractive, and everything to do with how much she loved her friends and wanted the company to continue to succeed.

'And that's the only reason you agreed to this,' he

said in a deep voice, perfectly calling her bluff. Was she that obvious? Undoubtedly. Her lack of experience with men meant she had no idea how to conceal her feelings.

Fortunately, the car drew to a stop at that point and a moment later a man appeared, dressed in a smart navy-blue suit, opening the door.

He spoke in Greek, and Ares responded in English. 'Miss Jones will be joining me. Please have champagne brought to us after take-off.'

Bea stepped out of the car, her jaw dropping at the sight of a gleaming white aeroplane emblazoned boldly with the word 'Lykaios' down the side in bright red letters.

'Of *course* you have a private jet,' she said with a bemused shake of her head.

'It's a practical necessity. I travel a lot.'

She refused to be impressed. 'You know how bad they are for the environment, don't you?'

He gestured to the steps. 'I offset my footprint in other ways. The reality is, my schedule cannot be made to fit in with commercial airlines.'

A flight attendant stood at the top of the steps, wearing a navy-blue trouser suit with a crisp white shirt.

'Miss Jones,' she greeted, word apparently having reached her of the unexpected guest. 'Good evening, Mr Lykaios,' she added.

'*Yassou*, Andrea.' He put a hand in the small of Bea's back, the touch light and impersonal, yet nonetheless doing very personal things to her insides. Large leather seats were on either side of the aisle, then there was a bank of four facing each other. He indicated she should take one, which she did, spreading her skirt over her knees to conceal her shoes.

He sat opposite, one ankle crossed over his knees in a pose that was sexy and nonchalant and drew attention to his powerful legs. She'd realised he was wearing a tuxedo, of course, but, seeing him sitting directly across from her, the full impact of his appeal hit her like a freight train.

'You're quite ridiculously handsome, you know.'

He burst out laughing. 'Thank you, I think?'

'It's not really a compliment,' she hastened to assure him. 'Just an observation. I mean, you'd be crazy not to realise that.'

'I always thought looks were subjective?'

'Sometimes, but some people are just objectively attractive. It's a bone structure thing.'

'Is it?' he prompted, teasing her with his eyes and his tone.

'Absolutely. But don't worry, I've never really thought good looks were anything to write home about, so I'm not going to break our cardinal rule.'

'I'm glad to hear it.'

For the briefest moment, despite her best intentions, Bea's eyes dropped to Ares's broad chest. Her temperature spiked; her tummy flipped.

Andrea arrived, proffering two glasses of champagne, but Ares waved his away. 'Coffee, *efcharistó*.'

Bea took hers gratefully. She needed something to soothe her frazzled nerves. 'Your first language is Greek?'

He dipped his head in acknowledgement.

'Yet you speak English flawlessly. Did you study here in the UK?'

'No.'

'How did you learn to speak it so well?'

His lips twisted in a smile that hid emotions Bea couldn't interpret. 'Speaking many languages was somewhat of a survival skill. I got good, fast.'

She quirked her brows. 'I don't understand.'

'No,' he agreed calmly, watching as she sipped her champagne.

She let out an exasperated laugh as the engines began to roar beneath them, the plane starting to move down the runway. 'So what does it mean?'

He stood suddenly, filling the void between their seats with his large frame and masculine aura. He reached down, his eyes holding hers as he buckled her seatbelt into place, fastening it so it sat low on her hips.

She was breathless, completely unable to look away. 'I could have done that.'

He took his own seat again, fastening the seatbelt just before the plane took off, a rush of adrenalin flooding Bea as it often did when she flew.

Once they levelled off Andrea returned, brandishing a tray. The aroma of coffee hit Bea squarely between the eyes. There was a small plate on the side, with crescent-shaped biscuits topped with flaked almonds.

'After my grandfather died, my brother and I spent some time on the streets. We made our way to Athens, where tourists were plentiful. At first we begged—' he said the word with disdain and her stomach clenched for him, the pain he felt at admitting just that palpable

'—but once I had a decent command of English and Japanese I began to do odd jobs for the hotels. I earned a pittance—less than begging, most days—but I liked it far more.'

Bea found it hard to catch her breath. 'I had no idea. I presumed you were—'

'Go on,' he prompted.

She couldn't look at him. Shame at her preconception—her *mis*conception—made her mouth grow dry. 'I just presumed you'd had an easier journey to success.'

'You thought I'd been born into a wealthy family?'

'Honestly, yes.'

He laughed. 'Why?'

'Because you are *so* wealthy,' she said, gesturing around the plane by way of example. 'Amassing this kind of fortune, the empire you command, having come from what you've just described... How did you do that?'

'I was extremely well-motivated.' He lifted the plate, offering her the biscuits. 'Have one.'

She took a biscuit automatically. 'I love *kourabiedes*.'

'These are my pilot's grandmother's recipe,' he said with a smile that might have disarmed a less well protected heart.

She took a bite, moaning as the flavour infused her mouth. Almond essence, but not so much as to be overpowering, ran through her, sweet and addictive. The insides were a soft, melt-in-the-mouth consistency, while the top was crunchy, so the texture was a contradiction she longed to enjoy more of. The dusting of icing sugar on top was the *pièce de resistance*.

Closing her eyes to savour the flavour more fully, when Bea opened them it was to find Ares staring at her in a way that drove every thought from her head. The full force of his dynamic attention was focused on her lips, his own mouth held in a tight line, his pupils large in his stormy grey eyes, his body tense, as though holding himself absolutely still against his will.

She lowered the biscuit to her lap, her heart hammering against her ribs.

'You eat that biscuit as though you are making love to it.'

The husky words sent her nerve endings into overdrive. If he had any idea she'd never made love to anyone—man or biscuit—what would he say then? Panic flooded her body, awkwardness at her inexperience overpowering her. She dropped her eyes, staring at the floor.

'It's very good.'

'As all lovers should be,' he responded.

Bea wished the plane would somehow expel her onto a nice fluffy cloud she could hide out in and pretend that Ares Lykaios wasn't talking to her about lovers and sex.

'I'm sorry your childhood was so difficult.'

She risked a glance at him to find a speculative look in his eyes, as though she were a puzzle he wanted to make sense of.

'Another apology?' he murmured, but though it was in the tone of a joke, it wasn't. At least, humour wasn't flooding the air between them. Instead, there was a raw, sensual heat that pulsed with throbbing need.

'A turn of phrase, I suppose.' Her voice sounded

strangled. She cleared her throat. 'What other languages do you speak?'

He sipped his coffee, his eyes holding hers. His hands were so powerful-looking, and the cup so delicate, she had to fight an urge to tell him to be careful he didn't break it. She imagined a man like Ares might drink from a goblet cast from stone, rather than pretty white porcelain with a fine gold rim. He replaced it on the tray, the action accompanied by a musical sound.

'Italian, French, Spanish. Some conversational Cantonese.'

She blinked at him, lifting her fingers and counting. 'Plus Greek, English and Japanese… That's six and a half languages.'

He crossed his legs, his foot brushing hers, sending arrows of desire through her body.

'Yes.'

'And you speak them fluently?'

'I couldn't write a novel in all of them, but I can hold a conversation like this.'

'You make me feel quite inadequate. I speak passable enough French to order my favourite meal in a restaurant, and that's about it.'

His smile sent butterflies into her belly. 'Which is?'

'Duck à l'orange.'

Something like approval glimmered in his eyes.

'I first had it when I was about twelve. I remember the trip so clearly.' She didn't go into the details— Paris Fashion Week, her mother's doting on the twins and their matching couture, Bea just growing into her hormonal body, feeling too big and too awkward, the photos the media had picked up of her bored, slouching, reading a book in the light cast by the stage. She pushed those sharp recollections away. 'We went to a restaurant and the waiter recommended it to my dad. He ordered one and so I thought I would too.'

Inwardly she grimaced, remembering her mother's displeasure. *'Darling, duck is incredibly fattening. And as for the sauce—'*

'It was so good. I made a point of ordering it from then on, whenever we ate out.' And not just to spite her mother, though that didn't hurt.

'If only we were going to Paris instead of Venice. I know the best restaurant, on a small cobbled street in Montmartre. It isn't famous, and has no Michelin stars or other plaudits, but the chef cooks traditional food as her father taught her to: each dish is perfection.'

'I'll have to get the name from you,' Bea said, more captivated than she cared to acknowledge by the image he was evoking.

'The restaurant is tiny. If you wish to try it, let me know and I'll arrange things. Ordinarily you have to book in months ahead.'

Bea hid a smile behind her glass of champagne. 'But, let me guess…for you, the chef makes an exception?'

He grinned that charming smile of his, pushing back in his chair and regarding her with all of his focus. 'Always. And therefore for you too, if I ask it of her.'

Bea had been to Venice a handful of times, always with her family, and when she was much younger. She'd been too caught up in the push and pull of their dynamic to enjoy the place fully, and certainly to appreciate its beauty. As the plane began to circle the curious, ancient water city with its glistening canals and baroque homes, she craned closer to the window, pressing her brow to the glass so she could see it better.

The sun was low in the sky, not yet disappeared but obliging with an incredible palette of golden lights. Rays of orange burst towards them, and she sighed, something like calm settling over her.

As the plane touched down, she avoided looking in Ares's direction for fear the sight of him might diminish even the beauty of the spectacular sunset.

CHAPTER FOUR

'PUT THIS ON.' He held out a fine silk scarf towards Bea, pale pink and turquoise, unmistakably designer.

Bea frowned, looking down at her outfit with a frown. 'Why?'

He focused on her hair then lifted the scarf, wrapping it over her head, letting the ends drape behind her. His hands fussed to ensure it was tightly tucked and then he nodded, stepping back to admire his work. 'So you don't get windswept.'

Bea turned to follow his gaze towards a low black speedboat.

Of course it made sense, yet, years earlier, her family had taken a taxi to the airport, not travelled by water despite being in Venice.

With a sensation of fluttering nerves, she put her hand in Ares's so he could hand her down onto the boat. A man stood, wearing jeans and a dark shirt, a lightweight cardigan over the top and a beret on his head.

'Enrico,' Ares greeted, following Bea into the boat with a lithe motion. The engine purred beneath them and the sun cast spots of gold across the water as it dipped nearer to the horizon.

It was a warm enough evening but, as the boat began to move, Ares shrugged out of his tuxedo jacket, holding it towards Bea. She shook her head instinctively, afraid to be engulfed in something that was still warm from his body, terrified of being wrapped in his masculine aroma. Ares, though, wouldn't take no for an answer. Perceiving the fine goosebumps on her arms, he slipped the jacket over her shoulders, his hands lingering there a second longer than might have been, strictly speaking, necessary.

Bea concentrated on remembering that he was the most important client the firm had, and he was annoyed at having been let down. *That* was the only reason she'd accepted this proposition.

'Would arriving alone to the ball really have been so bad?' she prompted, having to shout above the roaring wind.

His eyes probed hers, his smile a sensual lift of one side of his lips. 'I prefer having company.'

'You're the opposite to me,' Bea said with a small smile, turning away from him. She presumed the boat would swallow her words, but if she'd stayed looking at him she would have seen a speculative glint ignite in Ares's eyes.

Murano was recognisable first, the low-set red and brown buildings familiar to Bea from a long-ago trip to a glass factory there. A few minutes later and the boat tacked south, then swept into a wide canal surrounded on both sides by Gothic-style buildings, the Moorish influence apparent in the curved windows and ornate decorative screens. She held her breath as they passed beneath a bridge, tourists above it waving and smiling. She waved back then looked to Ares instinctively to find his eyes trained on her. He hadn't waved at them.

She felt gauche and silly, focusing instead on the view ahead. Enrico, the driver, reached the Grand Canal, pausing to allow a water taxi to pass, then several gondolas, before he pushed across, moving in a northerly direction. She didn't need to ask where the ball was being held. A few hundred metres away stood a grand old palace, peach in colour with white detailing and a red tiled roof. Several balconies were adorned with candelabras and musicians playing string instruments, so the sound of an orchestra filled the canal. A crowd had formed out the front, including a group of paparazzi.

Instincts honed long ago fired to life. She straightened her spine and squared her shoulders, but it did little to quell the flipping in her belly. How she hated the press!

Ares's hand in the small of her back didn't help. Enrico slowed down the boat, pulling in behind another speedboat which was disposing of its elegant guests, a similarly attired driver helping them onto the platform. Ares moved to stand in front of Bea, his fingers working at the scarf until it was freed, but he didn't move away. He stood in front of her, staring at her, reading her, watching her, so her lungs refused to work properly and all she could do was watch him right back.

'Am I—?' She frowned, painfully aware of how

often she'd let her mother down at events like this, and not wanting to do the same to Ares tonight. 'Do I look okay?'

His face bore a mask of confusion. 'Okay? Have I not already told you that you are beautiful?'

She shook her head, brushing aside his praise. 'I'm serious, Ares. I haven't been to anything like this in years.'

'Why not?'

Heat infused her cheeks. How to answer that? 'There hasn't been the need.' Her voice held a warning note.

'You look almost perfect.' He dropped the scarf onto a nearby seat, then put his hands on her lapels.

'Oh.' Belatedly she remembered that he'd provided his tux jacket for her to stay warm. 'Yes, of course.' She shrugged out of it as he slid it from her, standing where he was as he replaced it on his body. His scent still lingered though, and he stood close enough that his warmth did too. Enrico lurched the boat forward as space became available and Bea almost fell—she would have done so, had it not been for Ares's lightning-fast instincts. He shot out a hand, catching her behind the back, his legs like two powerful trunks securing them both to the centre of the boat, his body rigid as he drew her to him. It was the work of an instant, a quick movement to steady her, then he stepped away again, giving Enrico space to throw some ropes to staff atop the platform. The action drew the boat closer, and then Ares was holding out a hand to help Bea off.

She felt strangely shy as she put hers in his, glad when she reached relatively dry land and could relinquish his hand. The pins and needles stayed. Ares practically leaped from the boat, his natural athleticism easy to appreciate.

The sight of him was distracting enough that for a moment Bea didn't realise the photographers' lenses were trained on them—or rather, him—but when they began to call his name she instinctively shrank away, seeking to put distance between them.

Except Ares was too quick for that. His arm curved around her waist, drawing her to his side, fitting her perfectly against the muscular strength of his body, so that, despite the horrible feeling of being photographed, she was reassured by his proximity. Her mother's voice crashed into Bea's mind.

'Smile, darling. But don't show your teeth—your jawline is very horse-like. Straighten those shoulders—never hunch!'

It was over blessedly fast. Another boat pulled up, carrying a bona fide Hollywood celebrity, so Bea and Ares were allowed to walk in peace towards the double doors at the entrance to the famous palazzo. Hewn from ancient timber, thick enough to withstand any number of attacks, they were held open and guarded on either side by staff dressed in white tuxedo tops and slim-fitting black trousers. As they crossed the threshold, Bea used the move inside as an excuse to put some space between herself and Ares. After all, this wasn't a date.

The look he threw her was laced with mockery.

'This way.' He gestured across the tiled entranceway to a room that had Bea gasping at its splendid beauty. Paintings adorned the walls, either late Renaissance or

Baroque, swirling scenes with clouds and angels, rippling torsos and long white-bearded men brandishing golden spears to offset the panel framing, which was a lustrous golden colour. Candelabras adorned the walls and ceilings, the floor was a polished parquetry. The room was filled with guests dressed in the most incredible ballgowns and tuxedos, so Bea was glad she'd dusted off the dress she'd bought for one of her parents' Christmas parties in the hope of fitting in.

'This is a lot of people,' she remarked grimly.

'Yes.' His eyes skimmed hers speculatively; trembles ran the length of her spine.

'I've never seen anything so beautiful,' she murmured as they moved through the crowd. He dipped his head closer to hers so that he could hear her better. People were staring at them. She felt a familiar prickling sensation on the back of her neck, aware that, as they cut through the elegantly dressed guests, heads were turning, scanning Ares first and then Bea, appraising her in a way that filled her veins with ice. She moved a little to the side, putting even more distance between them.

She didn't belong with him. She wasn't good enough for him.

It was just like being with her picture-perfect adoptive family. Bea was an outsider.

A waiter passed with a tray of drinks and Bea swiped a glass of champagne from it, her large hazel eyes almost the colour of burned caramel in the atmospheric lighting.

'Why did you bring me here tonight?'

His expression was quizzical. 'We covered this. I didn't want to arrive alone.'

She waved a hand through the air. 'Fine. But surely there are dozens of women who would have jumped at the chance to be your date?'

His lips flattened into a line that spoke of disapproval at her questions.

'So why not ask one of them?' she insisted.

'Because I do not want any complications.'

She frowned. 'What does that mean?'

He lifted his shoulders in a laconic shrug. 'It means that I didn't particularly want a date on my arm, just a companion. No expectations, no promises. No…romance.'

She nodded thoughtfully. 'And any woman you asked would have expected more from you?'

He grimaced. 'There is always that risk.'

'So you don't date?'

He nodded once. 'I date. But not in the way you might expect.'

She laughed unexpectedly. 'How many ways are there?'

His look was droll. 'There is dating because you believe in the fairy tale, and there is dating because you enjoy companionship and sex.'

Heat burst through her. She found it impossible to breathe.

'And I only do the latter.'

Bea opened her mouth to say something but a man approached them at that exact moment, and she was immensely glad. It was clear that the gentleman—Ares referred to him as Harry—was intent on having an in-depth discussion with Ares about an investment in Argentina. Bea shifted sideways, more than happy to leave Ares be—and to get her head together.

Ever since he'd arrived to collect her, things had been spiralling wildly out of control and yet his assertion just now that he didn't welcome the complications of romance only served to reinforce the parameters of tonight. After all, they weren't dating in the hope of the fairy tale and she certainly wasn't going to have sex with him. Which meant this was business, pure and simple. She should have felt relieved by that, shouldn't she?

Ares had learned, with difficulty, to control his emotions. As a child he'd frequently felt lost, angry, hurt, damaged and broken, and as a teenager he'd been terrified but he'd known he couldn't reveal that to Matthaios, who'd depended on him for everything. He'd also realised that the more emotionally he behaved, the worse things got for them. He'd always been big for his age and the sight of a glowering, thundercloud-faced seventeen-year-old had hardly endeared them to the tourists they were depending on for small change. He could control his emotions with a vice-like skill, except recently.

Since Danica had come into his life he'd felt that control slipping, and tonight it was basically non-existent. He watched Bea walk away, catching the tiniest glimpse of her shoes as her skirts swished with her, and wishing more than anything that she'd stayed by his side. He'd liked the way she'd felt there, tucked against him, her softness the perfect antidote to his muscular strength. Instead, though, she weaved through the crowd; an irritating number of other women were wearing black so that, despite her height and natural grace, she disappeared from view far too quickly.

Between scanning the walls for the world class art and making sure she looked busy and distracted so as to avoid entreaties for conversation, Bea was also aware of a young girl with blonde ringlets and a pretty pale blue dress. She stood to the side of a gaily laughing group. From time to time she'd make a foray into the group, tugging on the skirt of one of the women, only to be rebuffed with a shake of the head and a pointed finger back to the wall.

'I didn't know there was going to be a real-life princess here!' Beatrice remarked as she drew closer.

The little girl—Bea would have guessed her age to be six or seven—had eyes that shone when they lifted to Bea's face. 'A real princess? Is there really?'

Bea feigned bemusement. 'Aren't I looking at one?'

'Where?' the little girl asked, craning her neck to see behind her.

'Here.' Bea gestured to the girl.

She looked surprised then shook her head. 'I'm not a princess.'

'Aren't you? You could have fooled me.'

Pink spots appeared on the girl's cheeks and then she was giggling. 'I'm American. We don't have princesses.'

'Hmm. Technically, I suppose you're right. Yet I could have sworn you were. Are you having fun, Your Highness?'

The little girl's smile brightened and then dipped away completely. 'Um…honestly?'

'Of course.'

'Not really.' She ran the toe of her shoe across the lines in the parquetry. 'I hate stupid balls. They're so boring.'

'They can be,' Bea agreed. 'Do you attend many?'

'Way too many,' the girl groaned. 'Dad's job means we always have to come and I hate them. There's never any other kids here and nothing for me to do but stand quietly and wait.'

Bea nodded sympathetically. 'I used to feel exactly the same way.'

'Really? My mom says I'm ungrateful. She says she would have loved to come to fancy parties at my age.'

Bea wrinkled her nose. 'Everyone's different, but I always found this sort of thing incredibly tedious.'

'Did you have to come when you were little?'

'Oh, yes, all the time.' Bea shuddered at the memories. 'To parties and shows and I would get bored and then so tired that sometimes I'd fall asleep on a chair in the corner!' she half joked.

'What happened?'

'They stopped bringing me,' she murmured, not mentioning that once the twins had been born she'd been shipped off to boarding school and only seen her adoptive parents a few weeks a year.

'I wish mine would stop bringing me,' the girl said a little too loudly, so her mother turned in preparation to scold her, pausing only when she saw Bea in conversation with the child.

'You know, I used to keep myself busy by playing maths games. Want me to show you what I mean?'

The girl nodded eagerly.

'Well, first of all, I'd count all the women wearing pink.' She frowned as she surveyed the crowd. 'There aren't very many tonight, so that won't take you long. Once you've done that, look for men wearing black shoes. Then women wearing tiaras, then men with ties versus bow ties. You'd be amazed at how it helps to pass the time.'

Having spent almost thirty minutes locked in conversation with Harry, expecting Beatrice to reappear at his side at any minute, he'd moved beyond frustration and onto irritation when she seemed to have simply disappeared into thin air.

He'd circumnavigated the room for another twenty minutes, being interrupted too many times to count to make short conversation with acquaintances and business contacts. As he'd scanned the room, his eyes had landed on something that made very little sense, and he'd drawn his gaze back.

A woman sitting on the ground at a ball was a strange sight indeed, so he knew somehow instinctively that it could only be Bea. Sure enough, as he moved closer, assiduously avoiding several more attempts to draw him into conversation, he saw that she wasn't, in fact, sitting so much as crouching beside a little girl, who was cross-legged beside her. They were staring into the crowd, a matching expression of concentration on their faces. Bea pointed at something and the little girl frowned as she followed the gesture, then she burst out laughing.

Something grabbed at his chest at the unexpected

sight and his impatience changed gear. No longer irritated by her disappearance, he was now irritated by the fact that there were so many people surrounding them when he wanted to be all alone with her.

It was a warning bell he heeded. He hadn't brought Bea to be distracted by her. He'd been honest with her earlier when he'd explained that he didn't want any complications. Perhaps ending this night prematurely was the wisest course of action.

'Ares—' she smiled to cover the rapid beating of her heart as she stood up '—there you are.'

'You sound as though you've been looking for me, but I suspect this is not the case.'

A guilty heat stole along her cheeks. 'You were busy,' she explained, fidgeting her hands in front of her.

'Yes. Harry is a partner in a project—'

'In Argentina, I gathered.'

'Indeed.'

'Who's this?'

Bea turned to the little girl. 'Emily, this is a friend of mine. Ares Lykaios, this is Her Royal Highness Princess Emily of Connecticut.'

'Hello, Your Highness,' he volleyed back without missing a beat. 'I'm pleased to meet you. Thank you for keeping Bea entertained while I was talking to someone else.'

'You're welcome.' Emily grinned. She pointed to his shoes. 'Thirty-nine!'

Bea nodded. 'You're right! Well done.'

'Are you enjoying yourself?' Ares asked.

Bea smiled at Emily. 'We're having a good time, aren't we?'

Emily nodded. 'Much better.'

Ares compressed his lips. Children made him uneasy; they always had done. Bea, on the other hand, seemed completely at ease with this little person. 'We can leave any time. If you're ready?'

Bea's eyes lit up. 'Really? You don't have to stay?'

'No. I've made an appearance; that's all that was expected of me.'

She looked down at Emily apologetically.

'It's okay.' The little girl pressed her hand to Bea's. 'I'll be fine. I'm looking for wigs next.' Emily wiggled her pale eyebrows so Bea laughed softly.

'That's a delicate one. Make sure you don't point or count too loudly.'

Emily tapped the side of her nose. 'Promise.'

Ares's hand was firmly insistent as he guided Bea away from Emily. 'A friend of yours?'

'A new friend.' Bea sighed. 'A lovely little girl rather too young to be dragged to events like this.'

'It's not exactly a child-focused evening.'

'She reminds me of how much I used to hate this kind of thing,' Bea said with a shiver.

'Used to?' he prompted, and again she was struck by how insightful he was.

'You caught me. I still do, generally speaking. In fact, you'd normally have to drag me kicking and screaming to something like this, so you should take it as an indication of how important your business is to the London Connection that I'm here with you tonight.'

She wondered why the words felt slightly disingenuous. As if to prove that he knew she was lying, he lifted a hand, catching a thick wave of brown hair and tucking it behind her ear. A *frisson* of awareness shimmied down her spine.

She gulped, trying to remember what she was saying, desperately hoping her voice emerged with a semblance of control.

'As a child, I was made to attend so many functions with my parents. Parties like this, with fancy clothes and beautiful music, and I came to hate them. Everything about them. The food, the forced laughter, the social interactions.' She lifted her shoulders. 'Give me a good book and a quiet living room and I'm all set.'

'And do you wish you were in your living room now, instead of here?'

The challenge lay between them. She feared they both knew the answer to that…

'I…am having a better time than I anticipated,' she said unevenly.

It was like stepping off the edge of a cliff and into an abyss. She was in freefall, losing herself in the depths of his silver-grey eyes, with nothing to hold onto. He stared at her long and hard and turned away from her, but not before he uttered under his breath, 'As am I.'

CHAPTER FIVE

THE GONDOLA HAD been a mistake. He should have refused. But her eyes had been so hopeful as she'd looked out on the canal, watching the little boats bobbing past, and before he'd been able to stop himself Ares had heard himself say, 'Would you like to take a ride?'

Of course, he'd simply been being polite. She'd smiled awkwardly and for a moment he'd held his breath, thinking she'd say no, but then she'd nodded, a simple shift of her head.

It was tighter than he'd imagined in the boat, the seat designed for lovers, so they had no choice but to sit hip to hip, her body lightly pressed to his side, her warmth permeating him. 'You're good with children.' The words were cool, and he was glad. This wasn't a date—she wasn't a woman he was looking to bed.

'Thank you.'

Silence stretched between them, long and taut. He should continue it, ignore her, get this evening over. But again, almost against his volition, he asked, 'Do you have siblings?'

Her smile seemed to communicate something he

couldn't understand. Uncertainty? Pain? 'My adoptive parents had twin girls when I was seven. Annelise and Amarie.'

'So you must have been given plenty of opportunities to babysit?' The moon overhead was almost completely full, only a fingernail snippet missing from one side. It cast the canals of Venice in a glorious silver light, the water lapping gently at the edges of the wooden boat.

'I went to boarding school shortly after the girls were born. I really only saw them during the holidays—a few weeks a year at most.' Her words were robotic, as though she'd practised the line many times.

'How old were you when you were adopted?'

Her fingers fidgeted in her lap; she stared down at them, the matte black nail polish the perfect complement to her dress. 'Three.'

He waited for her to continue and was eventually rewarded with a shaky explanation.

'Ronnie and Alice tried to fall pregnant for a long time. Years and years of IVF and fertility treatments, all with no luck. Adoption was their last resort—definitely not the kind of parenthood Alice had envisaged, but better than nothing.'

Ares was very still, the rejection she was describing making him pity the little girl she'd been.

'The twins were a miracle. She was in her forties when she conceived, and without fertility assistance, after years of being told it would never happen. You can imagine how doted on the girls were.'

'And you felt pushed aside?'

Bea's smile was iced with years of pain. 'I felt that

way because I was.' She fixed him with a gaze that was like steel, and yet it didn't deter him. He could see through it easily. 'Anyway, I don't really like to talk about my family.'

But he wouldn't let her turn away. His finger caught her chin, guiding her face back to his, and now he was so close to her, grey eyes morphing to silver in the moonlight reading her as he had been all evening. What the hell was he doing? She was pushing him away with her words, and he should let her do exactly that. Not caress her face and draw her towards him. 'Families can be complicated.' His voice was throaty.

'Yes.' Just a whisper, the word caught on the air, brushing across his cheek towards his ear. She was a beautiful woman, but he hadn't brought her to Venice with this in mind. Yet sitting in the gondola, his body so close to hers, he felt a drugging desire to throw sense to the wind and act as though she was any other woman. What harm could come from that?

'Amy and Clare are my family.' It was a strange thing to say. Was she simply explaining that she didn't need her adoptive parents and siblings? Or was she looking to remind him—and herself—of her best friends and business partners?

The gondola moved to the side to let another boat past, and some waves formed in its wake that caused the craft to rock from side to side, lurching Bea towards Ares. She made no attempt to resist the gravitational movement and he was glad.

Her hands lifted to his shirt; her face stayed tilted to his.

He stared at her, torn between doing the right thing and getting the hell back to Enrico and sending her back to London, or doing what he desperately wanted and closing the distance between them completely. His eyes dropped to her lips, staring at their pouting form, aching for her. She lifted one finger to her mouth, tracing the line his eyes were taking, her fingertip trembling at the intimate gesture. It was an invitation and an entreaty; what she wanted was blatantly obvious.

And so? Why fight this? He'd explained to her that he didn't believe in romantic relationships. He'd been explicit in telling her that all he looked for when he dated a woman was sex. If she was interested in him, and what he was offering, then he'd be a fool to resist. Right?

'Tell me, Bea, did you have a rule about kissing?'

Her breath hitched in her throat at his low-voiced question. She tried to think straight but it was almost impossible. 'We agreed no kissing.'

'I think you said no touching too,' he suggested, dropping the hand that held her chin to her knee, where he cupped her flesh there, sending sharp arrows of pleasure through her skin. She leaned infinitesimally closer to him, her skin lifting in a veil of goosebumps.

'And definitely no flirting.'

'Tell me, Counsellor, how does one go about revising the rules?' he asked.

Her mouth was drier than dust. She was on the precipice again, nudging closer to the edge even when she knew she should turn and walk away.

'You're a client,' she reminded herself and him, saying the words aloud in a desperate attempt to bring sanity back to her mind.

'Not tonight.' His head dropped closer to hers, so close that if she pushed up she could take his lips for her own. Blood formed a pounding cacophony in her ears, an orchestra of need like a tidal wave she was cresting over.

'No? What are you then?'

She sucked in a gulp of breath but the stars in her eyes didn't go away.

'They are your rules,' he responded without answering directly. 'To break or ask me to abide by. I'm in your hands.'

The imagery conjured was too much. How could she explain to someone like Ares Lykaios that she was nothing like his usual companions? How could she explain to him that she didn't simply go on dates with handsome strangers and kiss them beneath the bright Venetian moonlight? How could she explain to him that she was, of all things, a twenty-nine-year-old virgin?

'I don't think this is a good idea,' she whispered. Because surely whatever happened next would be wildly disappointing for him—and possibly earth-shattering for her. The imbalance in their experience was terrifying. 'I'm really, really not your type.'

Despite the tension thickening between them, his smile reached inside and calmed Bea's nerves. Her body was, if anything, moving closer to his.

'If you want to retain our original agreement, then I'll respect that. But make the choice based on *your* feelings, not what you believe mine to be. I know exactly what I want right now.'

Her heart lurched completely off-balance. 'And that is?'

He moved so close that their lips brushed and whatever willpower she had left to resist him disappeared completely. 'I want to spend the night with you.' His finger ran along her cheek, and she was trembling against his body, the desire he was invoking too much to resist. 'Just one night, nothing more.'

It sounded so simple! So easy! Sex, plain and simple—except nothing with Ares Lykaios would ever be plain.

'But I'm—' The words trailed into nothing.

Then, to hell with the rules, he was kissing Bea and she was kissing him back, their lips enmeshed in a way that blew all Bea's preconceptions of such a thing well out of the water. Unlike the passionless encounters she'd had in the past, every movement of his mouth stirred flame in her blood, so that she couldn't sit still. If she did, the fire would engulf her; she had to move.

The boat rocked from side to side as she pushed up into his lap, needing to be closer to him, so much closer than their clothes and public location allowed. His hands moved inside his jacket that she wore, wrapping around her slender waist, holding her there as he drove his tongue into her mouth, the rhythm fast and urgent, leaving her in no doubt as to just how badly he did, in fact, want her. One hand on her hip moved lower, cupping her bottom, and she groaned, flinching a little at the completely foreign contact but welcoming it too, needing it—and him—in a way that shook her to the core of her being.

She often felt too tall, too ungainly, but in Ares's hands she was dainty and petite, his size engulfing her, his strength dominating her completely as he shifted and by degrees moved her with him, so she was straddling him, the voluminous skirts of her dress forming a circle around them, her fingers pushing through his hair and joining behind his neck, her breasts crushed to his chest as his mouth continued to torment hers, his expertise and experience meaning that the kiss alone had the power to make her stomach swoop all the way to her toes.

But then he rolled his hips, lifting a little on the seat of the gondola, so she felt something unfamiliar and unmistakable between her legs, his hard arousal striking panic into her heart even as ancient feminine instincts came to the fore, reassuring her that she'd know what to do when the time came. Her hand dropped to his shoulder, then lower still to his shirt, her fingers curling into the fabric and squeezing, holding on tight.

He tore his mouth away but held her head steady where it was, calling Italian words over his shoulder.

He was kissing her again before she could ask him what he'd said, but the gondolier took a side canal, so she could only presume Ares had given a change of course. And, with any luck, to a hotel!

Why was it that he, of all people, could affect her like this? She'd spent her entire adult life believing she was immune to the opposite sex and yet here he was, stirring her to a fever pitch on a boat in the middle of Venice.

'To hell with the rules,' he growled.

His hand pushed under the fabric of her dress, resting on her thigh. He kept it there, not pushing higher, as though he sensed it was a limit for her, that she needed time to process that sensation first, to reconcile herself to the intimacy before he took another. And God, she hoped he would take another and another and another. Sparks of anticipation flew through Bea's blood as she realised what was about to happen: Finally, she was going to have sex. She was going to lose her virginity, so she could have some understanding of what all the fuss was about. And with Ares Lykaios she knew it would be a night to remember!

A low, throbbing noise was sounding in her ears, running through her body, vibrating in her chest. She attributed it to her heart until her brain kicked into gear. Pulling back from him and staring—dazed—into his hooded grey eyes, she pressed a hand to his torso. 'You're ringing.'

He looked as swept up by passion as she felt. He stared at her for a beat before the words resulted in action. He lifted his shoulders, pulling her closer. 'I don't care.'

She moaned softly as he parted her lips with his, sliding his tongue in more slowly this time, the enquiry gentle, but no less urgent. She rolled her hips, a primal wisdom beating in her heart, showing her how to answer her needs, how to act.

The throbbing began once more, vibrating through Bea's chest, so she pushed away, her breath laboured, her eyes sparkling. 'Answer it, then switch the damned thing off.'

His brows flexed and with a forceful exhalation he reached into his pocket. A frown crossed his face as he glanced at the screen, and then he swiped it to answer, his other hand still on her thigh, his thumb stroking gently over the skin there, as though he knew he could keep her in his sensual thrall with that slight contact alone.

'Yes?' Frustration emerged in the clipped tone, taking Bea back to their first meeting, when he'd spoken to her like that. She was glad not to be on the receiving end of his impatience any more, and pitied whoever had called.

They were in close proximity and she could hear the string of high-pitched words without being able to understand any of them, owing to the language in which they were being spoken. His thumb stopped moving; the weight of his hand on her thigh grew lighter.

He barked something into the phone in Greek, his eyes on Bea's face without, she suspected, seeing her. Ares was gentle yet insistent as he dislodged her from his lap, shifting her back to the seat at his side, his features looking as carved from granite as ever but harsher now so they were jagged and sharp. For no reason she could think of, a shiver ran down Bea's spine.

He said something short and then disconnected the phone. It was the only movement he made; the rest of him was completely still. Shocked? She couldn't tell. It only lasted a small beat of time and then he was speaking to the gondolier once more.

'Ares? What is it?' Her voice was still husky, the passion flooding her veins slow to recede.

When he looked at her it was almost as though he'd forgotten she was there. 'Beatrice,' he muttered. Her heart lurched. She'd been treated as an inconvenience often enough to immediately understand his meaning.

'I have to return home, immediately. It cannot be delayed.'

Concern eclipsed her own feelings of rejection. 'Has something happened?'

A grimace was his only response. Mentally she derided herself for asking such a stupid question. *Obviously* something had happened. But what?

Everything felt different now. The buildings of Venice still sat on either side of the canal but now it was as though they were looming watchfully, bathed in too-bright yellow rather than a gentle gold, and even the lapping of the water seemed to inflame Bea's uncertainties and anxieties.

They had not travelled far and, using a series of shortcuts, the gondolier had them back at the speedboat a short time later. He pulled up to the pontoon, moving to help Bea disembark, but Ares was there first, his strong hand guiding her out of the boat even as his face bore an unrecognisable mask of stony intent. Another shiver spread through her as she shrugged out of his jacket and looked around behind her.

'You go.' She nodded towards the sleek black speedboat. 'I'll catch a water taxi to a hotel.'

His frown was just the slightest shift of his lips, then his hand was on her back, drawing her with him. 'I doubt any will have space available. Between the ball and the opera, Venice is packed.'

'Surely somewhere—'

'Nowhere reputable.'

She nodded, relying on his better knowledge of Venice at that point, stepping into the speedboat with him. At the airport, she could arrange a flight to London. Disappointment was a visceral ache rapidly spreading through her. She refused to think about where the night had been heading only moments earlier; she refused to think about the heat still pooling in her abdomen, demanding fulfilment. She refused to imagine Ares naked on top of her, and what the weight of his body would feel like over hers; she refused to go down that path even when it was dragging at her every second of the torturous, silent boat ride to the airport.

Relief flooded Bea's veins when they arrived; she wanted Ares more than she could say, but at the same time she desperately needed to get away from him so she could process what had just happened.

He walked quickly away from the speedboat and she had to take long strides to keep up. He was taking the same path they'd trodden earlier—a partly concealed sign declared *'Aerei Privati'*. Private Aircraft.

She stopped walking and, despite the fact he was marginally ahead of her, some sixth sense must have alerted him to the change because he halted and turned to her. 'Come. I must be quick.'

His accent was more noticeable, his words rushed with something like panic.

'You go on. I'll make my way to the terminal and see about getting a ticket to London.'

His brow furrowed, as though he hadn't expected that. 'There won't be any commercial flights at this time.'

Beatrice glanced at her wristwatch, groaning because of course that was true! It was almost midnight. She looked around with a growing sense of unease. 'Then an airport hotel—' She gestured to a low building in the distance bearing a familiar logo, associated with three-star hotels the world over.

'No.'

She startled at the word. 'I beg your pardon?'

He compressed his lips, turning to her in a manner that made Bea feel as if she were a recalcitrant child. She stood her ground.

'I do not have any time to spare, Beatrice. I cannot take you to that hotel, and I will not leave you to make your own way there. So you need to come with me.'

'Where to?'

'My home.'

'I don't even know where that is.'

'Does it matter?'

She glared at him with hauteur.

He sighed. 'In Greece. It is an emergency; I do not have time to argue with you.'

'Then don't argue with me,' she said quietly, practically on the brink of tears at how the night had turned out. 'You do your thing and I'll do mine. I'm a big girl, more than capable of getting myself to that hotel and checking in for the night.'

He shook his head. 'I won't have it on my conscience if something goes wrong, and I do not have the time to see you there safely myself.'

'We're going around in circles here, Ares, because I've already said I'll be fine, and you're saying you don't know that for sure. But I can see no reason to come with you, especially when something's obviously happened that requires your attention, so, short of kidnapping me, you're going to have to accept my decision.'

He stared at her, his bright eyes bitter; she could feel her skin burning under their assault. And then he moved, taking one step towards her and lifting her easily, as though she weighed nothing, hoisting her over his shoulder. She was too shocked to make a noise; he had already resumed his earlier path and taken several steps before she squawked in indignation, 'What the hell are you doing?'

'Kidnapping you.' The words obviously came from between gritted teeth. 'Just as you suggested.'

CHAPTER SIX

HE HAD TO give his flight crew credit. They acted as though seeing him arrive hauling a very cross woman over one shoulder was a totally everyday occurrence, running through all the normal pre-flight checks without batting an eyelid. For his part, Ares was grateful for their professionalism, and only slightly shocked by his own behaviour towards Bea.

It hadn't been about wanting to kidnap her and drag her to his home, even though such thoughts had been tormenting him all evening, so that he'd imagined her against the sheets of his bed, her languorous hazel eyes staring up at him, begging him to make love to her.

This had been a question of practicality alone.

The call from his housekeeper, Xanthia, had pushed all other considerations aside. Cassandra, the nanny, had walked out after hours of the baby's screaming. Xanthia, herself a grandmother, had sounded beside herself. What choice did Ares have but to go straight home and assess the situation?

His eyes drifted to Bea, who was sitting opposite him, a belligerent expression on her face that—at any other time—he would have been very tempted to erase from her pretty features using far from respectable methods. As if to torment him even further, his fingers tingled with the memory of her silky-smooth thigh beneath his palm, the way she'd juddered at the contact, her body begging him for more.

He'd held back, telling himself they had all night, that the pleasure was better savoured than rushed, but now he wished he'd ignored that impulse and let his hand drift higher, finding her sweet femininity and brushing her there, feeling her heat and watching as she exploded in his arms.

'I wish you'd tell me what's happened,' she said quietly. 'It seems like the least you could do.'

It was the first time she'd spoken all flight, and they were almost in Athens. He stared at her, the words locked deep inside. But he had to say *something*. She was about to walk into a scene that would make it perfectly obvious he'd been left—literally—holding the baby.

'Five months ago, my brother's wife died.' He spoke clinically, no sign of the ensuing trauma in his words. 'It was a complete shock—something went wrong during childbirth. Ingrid was delivered of their baby, a little girl, but then wouldn't stop bleeding, and the doctors could do nothing to save her.'

Bea gasped in that way she had, lifting her fine-boned hand to cover her lips.

'Now my brother is…not well…' he glossed over the nature of Matthaios's illness out of instinct to protect him '…and has left me with the care of his child while he seeks treatment.'

The sympathy in her eyes was unmistakable. Ares hated it. As a teenager he'd seen that look on countless faces and he'd sworn he'd show them. He was not an object of pity. Strengthening his spine, he infused ice into his bones. 'Naturally, I hired an exceptional nanny. My workload is hardly conducive to the care of a child, and young children particularly need a lot of care. Unfortunately, the woman I hired has been almost as much work as my niece since day one. My housekeeper just called to inform me that the nanny had walked out.'

'Cassandra,' Bea prompted thoughtfully.

'How did you—?'

'She called while you were in Clare's office.' Pink bloomed in Bea's cheeks. He looked away, controlling his body's response to the betraying gesture with difficulty.

'Yes, Cassandra.' He spat the name with derision, almost missing the way Bea's lips lifted a little at the corners. She was smiling at him? Trying not to laugh at him? It didn't make sense and Ares liked things to make sense.

'I have to get back there, to see what's going on,' he snapped.

Her eyes, clear pools of burnt butter, appraised him for several seconds and then she nodded slowly. 'If you'd explained this sooner I wouldn't have fought you at the airport.'

His lips tugged downwards. 'It didn't occur to me. I was too preoccupied.'

Again, sympathy crossed her face. It took Ares a moment to realise it wasn't sympathy for him so much as for the unknown baby, and the entire situation.

'Naturally, I'll arrange for you to fly back to London tomorrow.'

She barely reacted, yet in the depths of her eyes he was sure he saw something unexpected—something akin to disappointment? Or maybe that was wishful thinking: ego?

'Don't worry about me,' she insisted quietly. 'I can take care of myself.'

Bea's adoptive parents owned a grand old country home in the English countryside, the kind of place with rolling green lawns, a stream filled with trout, stables that had been empty for many years until the twins asserted a desire to learn to ride, and horses were therefore acquired from top breeders. The desire had lasted three weeks, the horses longer—they were now given free rein of the western paddocks and, from time to time, found their way into the orchard and ate their body weight in fruit, much to Alice Jones's displeasure. As an organic-only fruitarian, the orchard represented almost her sole source of food, so the horses' act had been seen as a declaration of war.

The house itself dated to the early Tudor period, though much modernisation had occurred in recent years, and now boasted ten bedrooms, each with its own bathroom, three swimming pools—one for diving, courtesy of Amarie's insistence that she was going to be an Olympic diver. The pool had been completed about a week too late—she'd moved onto playing the drums by then and, despite the fact that Ronnie had a full studio in the basement of the house, a separate drums studio was built for Amarie, perhaps to save Ronnie from the torture of listening to her murder the tempo of any more classic rock music.

So it wasn't as though Beatrice hadn't been surrounded by wealth. But ever since arriving at the airport in London and being ushered into Ares's private jet she'd felt as though she'd been exposed to a whole other level of extravagance. Upon touching down in Athens they were ushered to a limousine which drove them a very short distance to a gleaming black helicopter with darkly tinted windows. The upholstery was brown leather and the details oak. Her companion was as silent as a tree himself and his manner became colder, more intimidating with every minute that passed.

Bea distracted herself by staring out of the window, trying not to compare him to the way he'd been on the gondola. Then, she'd almost felt as though she could say anything to him, tell him anything, but now he was so distant it was impossible to think of him as anything except an incredibly successful self-made businessman who was also a very important client—a man whose business the London Connection needed to retain.

And, for some reason, all she could think about was the time she'd been sent home from school with suspected chickenpox and somehow the message had never reached her parents. The doors to the house had been locked—Bea never had a key of her own—and so she'd walked around to the drawing room, peering in through the windows. The sight of her parents and sisters having dinner together had made her heart ache in an unforgettable way. It had been easy to lie to herself until that night, to make excuses for why she was treated one way and her sisters another, but seeing them enveloped in the warmth of their home, the focus of such obvious parental love, had made the literal point to Bea that she was an outsider.

It had made her see that she had never had that. Not from her biological parents, and not from the parents who'd adopted her. No one had ever wrapped her into their warm embrace and made her feel as though she was special and irreplaceable.

She'd never looked to her family for affection again, nor did she seek it from anyone else. Being on her own was better, easier and infinitely safer.

The helicopter circled lower to the ground. The full moon shone on the coastline, showing the ocean as a shimmering expanse of black with a silver trail through its centre and, along the shore, set several miles apart, a handful of houses. The helicopter headed towards one that was boxy and modern, elegant lighting illuminating the sides in a warm glow that was somehow at odds with the stark white walls. A swimming pool was lit with turquoise lights, lending it the impression of a five-star resort. The helicopter came lower, confirming the fact that this was Ares's house, landing squarely on the rooftop.

The helicopter had barely touched down before he had unbuckled his seatbelt and was standing, moving to the door at the side. Bea couldn't take her eyes from him. He was completely absorbed, focused only on reaching home and finding out what had happened. She unbuckled her own seatbelt, the fierce throb of disappointment in her body not worthy of her in that moment. There were far greater things to worry about.

'What happened?' he demanded as he moved from the stairs and into the living room. He had to speak loudly to be heard above the infant's screaming. Every two seconds the little baby paused to suck in a gulp of air, then made a bubbling sound as she pushed it out, wailing into the night. If he allowed himself to feel fear he knew it would overtake him, so he refused to admit the possibility that something could be physically wrong with Danica. Not on his watch.

'She will not stop crying,' Xanthia said in Greek.

Despite the fact he'd barely spoken to her since leaving Venice, Ares was ever conscious of Bea just behind him, and switched effortlessly to English. 'What caused this?'

'Nothing.' Xanthia did the same, herself fluent in many languages, a prerequisite to the job as he required his housekeeper to oversee the management of his properties in various countries. 'She had a bath and then refused her evening meal. When Cassandra attempted to put her to bed she began to wail, and nothing could calm her.'

'Why?' he asked with obvious disbelief. 'Shouldn't she be tired?'

Xanthia pursed her lips and looked at him as though he were an idiot and, to be fair, in that moment he felt like one. But shouldn't this be easy? Weren't babies supposed to just need food and sleep?

He ground his teeth together, the sense of inadequacy overwhelming. 'For God's sake, has she been like this the whole time?'

'Yes,' Xanthia confirmed, rocking the baby from side to side, which only caused Danica to scream more loudly.

'You said she didn't eat—' the voice came from behind him '—could she be hungry?'

Xanthia's green eyes turned to Bea, appraising her quickly. 'She is only little. Dinner consists of some spoons of cereal and a bottle of milk.'

'Nonetheless,' Bea continued, moving towards the baby. Despite the screams, the gentle rustle of her skirts reached his ears, reminding him of the way they'd felt bunched in his hands. He formed a fist at his side, an act of determination, a refusal to be distracted by his body's base impulses. Bea lifted a hand to the baby's head, checking for a temperature.

'She's warm,' Bea said gently. 'But that's probably because she's so agitated.' She held her hands out. 'May I?'

Xanthia's jaw dropped. 'Oh, please. I have been holding her for hours. Please, yes, take her.'

'Would you go and prepare her bottle?' Bea prompted, taking the baby and barely flinching at the noise. Without lifting her attention from Danica's face, she addressed him. 'Ares, I think a cool facecloth might help to calm her. Would you get one?'

He stared at her, totally unprepared for this turn of

events. He'd expected Bea to fade into the background at best, or, at worst, be something of an inconvenience if she'd continued to fight with him about coming to his home, but her cool manner and air of control knocked him sideways.

Even Danica seemed mildly less hysterical in Bea's arms.

'Yes, of course,' he said belatedly, turning on his heel to fetch what she'd asked for. He noticed as he waited for the cloth to dampen sufficiently that he wasn't wearing his tuxedo jacket. It was still wrapped around Bea's shoulders. The thought tightened his body, making him far more aware of her as a woman than was appropriate, given the circumstances.

He entered the lounge at the same moment Xanthia did, and both stopped walking and simply stared at each other.

Danica was silent. Not quite, he amended. She was making lots of little breathy noises, rapid and urgent, as she calmed down from so much screaming. Her cheeks were mottled pink and tear-stained, her hair damp from crying, her nose sticky with snot, but she was no longer wailing.

As he approached, he heard Bea's voice, soft and gentle, singing words in a language he didn't know, like English but different. Almost elvish, reminding him of Middle-Earth.

'Oh, my ears,' Xanthia whispered, smiling broadly, her dark grey hair piled high on her head in a loose bun, frazzled after hours of trying to console a screaming child.

He held out the facecloth to Bea but she shook her head. 'She's cooler now that she's stopped crying. Perhaps a tissue though?'

He nodded without moving, simply standing, awe-struck at the sight of someone so completely *comfortable* with the child. Not since Danica had arrived at his house had he seen her actually seem halfway to peaceful.

Xanthia held the bottle out to Bea. She took it, returning to singing as she looked around. Her eyes momentarily met Ares's and something passed between them, something fierce and intractable, a magnetic force that demanded acknowledgement. He ground his teeth together, jabbing one hand into his pocket.

'The tissue,' she reminded him with a pointed look and the hint of a smile, jolting him into action.

'Right, the tissue,' he repeated, still reluctant to leave the scene. He bypassed Xanthia, pausing beside her. 'You should go to bed. Thank you for holding the fort tonight. I'm in your debt.'

'Of course, Ares,' she said with a shake of her head, switching back to Greek. 'The poor little dove simply couldn't be settled. Not until you showed up with the baby whisperer. This nanny shows much more promise than the other.'

He was about to correct her but, instead, Xanthia's words settled inside his chest, landing there with a soft thud. *This nanny.* He cast a glance over his shoulder.

It was easy to see why Xanthia would have made that mistake. Despite her formal dress, Beatrice was unmistakably at home holding the baby…

* * *

'Where's her nursery?' she whispered, stroking the darling little infant's shoulder with the pad of her thumb.

Ares had been standing, watching for the twenty minutes it had taken to feed Danica and rock her slowly to sleep. 'I'll show you.'

Bea stood slowly—it had been years since she'd held a baby, though it was surprising to realise how easily it all came flooding back. Memories of helping her friend Priti with late-night feeds and colicky tantrums filled her with confidence. This, though, was different.

Holding Danica, feeding her, lulling her to sleep, had caused something to flicker to life inside Bea that had caught her completely off-guard. A stirring of maternal instincts she absolutely didn't expect and definitely didn't want. She'd decided a long time ago that she was *never* having children.

She walked beside him and, without the ticking time bomb of a furiously upset infant, was able to take in the details of his palatial home. It was a temple to modernity, all crisp white walls, polished cement floors with Danish-style furniture. The only concession to colour came in the form of abstract paintings which hung in niches along the walls, lit with art-gallery-style spotlights. The stairs were highly polished wood. As Ares walked ahead of her Bea had a perfect view of his powerful legs and firm bottom and the sight of both made her mouth go dry.

She looked away, concentrating only on her steps, one after the other, holding Danica close to her chest so that she would stay comforted and warm.

Ares paused on the landing, pointing to an open door a little down the hall. Bea walked towards it, trying not to speculate on which of these doors might lead to his room. The nursery was a guest bedroom with a cot in the corner and a rocking chair by the window. Bea stood above the cot for a moment, singing 'Calon Lân' to Danica, gently lowering her over the sheet. She startled a little, so Bea placed her on the mattress quickly then held her hand on Danica's tummy, reassuring her she was still there, lifting her fingers lightly, gradually, until it was clear that Danica had settled. She turned to Ares and smiled, overcome with shyness now, uncertain what to say.

Nothing within the baby's earshot, that was for sure! What the poor little thing needed more than anything was a good night's sleep.

As she stepped through the door, Ares pressed his hand to her back, guiding her towards the stairs. The lightest touch made her nerves go haywire. She moved a little ahead of him on the steps, her own hand seeking the reassuring firmness of the railing.

In the lounge, he strode across the room, throwing open the glass doors and quirking a brow by way of silent invitation. Bea hesitated a moment, then moved in his direction, keeping her face averted as she brushed past him.

It was cool outside; she was grateful to still have his jacket on. Salt filled the air; the sound of rolling waves made a gentle background rhythm.

'You're good with kids.'

She turned to face him, a tight smile on her face. 'She

was just overwrought. Babies don't always know how to calm themselves down; they need us to do it for them.'

He shook his head dismissively. 'The nanny I hired came highly recommended but she couldn't manage Danica. No one could.'

'I find that impossible to believe.'

'I'm not making it up.'

She tilted her head. 'I'm not saying that. It's just—she's just a baby, Ares. She's—did you say five months old?'

He nodded once.

'That's so little! And she's had a lot of change in her life so far. Babies are more perceptive than people realise.'

'And you are the only one who can calm her,' he said quietly.

'That's not true.'

'How did you know what to do?'

Her smile was tinged with the best kinds of memories—sweet ones, those that were solely good. 'When I was at university, my flatmate Priti fell pregnant. It was a one-night stand, completely unexpected. The dad wasn't in the picture. She really wanted to be able to keep studying and, seeing as we were doing the same course, we came up with a schedule for school work and baby-minding. It was a crazy time.' Bea laughed softly, recalling the madness of it. 'I'd go to lectures and record them for her, we'd cram over buckets of soaking laundry—nappies and bibs—and study while Nikki slept. She wasn't an easy baby. In fact, I'd say she was downright difficult. Some nights it would take hours to get her to sleep. *Hours*, no exaggeration. Some babies are just like that,' she said with a shrug.

When he didn't respond, she rushed to fill the silence. 'If it's any consolation, I can assure you that that difficult baby is now a confident, intelligent pre-teen who rarely has a temper tantrum and absolutely sleeps through the night, so it does get easier.'

Ares seemed to stiffen. 'Hopefully she won't be my problem for much longer.'

Bea's lips parted on a soft sound of outrage, her expression full of chastisement. 'That's no way to talk about your niece.'

He winced at the reprimand. 'Ever since she arrived she has been like this. Screaming. Red-faced. Angry.'

In spite of his words, Bea smiled. 'She wasn't angry. Misunderstood is a better way to describe her.'

'I paid a nanny to understand her.'

'It doesn't sound like that worked out very well.'

'Cassandra clearly wasn't the right choice.'

'Apparently not.'

The silence between them throbbed and every second that passed did something to Bea. She felt herself being pulled towards him, as though a ribbon was wrapped around her, dragging her closer. She resisted it, but the effort it took was monumental.

'My brother is likely to be in hospital for another few weeks.'

Bea frowned at the swift conversation-change.

'I need someone to help with Danica while she's with me.'

'Perhaps you can find a nanny who has more experience with unsettled babies? It's quite a specific skillset, but if you let the agency know—'

He shook his head, moving towards her with urgency. 'I'm not going to contact the agency again.'

Bea looked confused. 'Then how will you find someone?'

Ares pressed a finger to her lips, silencing her as he'd done in the office earlier that day. Had it really only been a day? 'I've already found her.'

Bea stared up at him, unable to think straight when he was so close.

'Danica is a difficult child, you're right. But you were able to calm her easily.'

'That's just experience.'

'It's experience I need.'

She stared up at him, her expression wary. He couldn't possibly be suggesting…? 'You do realise I have a job?'

His eyes glittered with ruthless determination. 'Unfortunately, *agápi mou*, you showed your hand too early.'

Bea was silent.

'We both know what my business means to the London Connection.'

Her heart stammered, her jaw dropping in surprise.

'And we both know you'll do almost anything to keep me happy.'

'Ares,' she whispered, a plea in her voice, 'I was happy to help you tonight, but I can't just walk out of my job—my real job—to play babysitter. No matter how cute the baby is.' Or how sexy the uncle, she added mentally.

'Unfortunately, I'm desperate. Otherwise I'd never think of blackmailing you into staying here for the month.'

'A *month*?' she repeated on a wave of something that was terrifyingly like excitement.

'My brother's treatment will take a few weeks, at least. Let's say a month, to be safe.'

'We can't "say" anything, Ares. I'm not agreeing to this.'

'Of course you are,' he dismissed easily. 'You have no choice.'

She shook her head.

He made a frustrated sound. 'I would prefer not to bully you into this, Beatrice. Stay because we—I—need your help. Because I must do whatever it takes to help Danica. Stay because it's the right thing to do, just like it was the right thing to help Priti finish her degree. Stay because I am desperate.' He moved closer, his body finishing the intoxicating job his words had started. 'Stay because you want to finish what we started on the boat tonight, and a month gives us ample time to do that.'

Her stomach squeezed on an exhilarating wave of hope and need, but her brain was reluctantly firing to life. Disbelief hit her. On the gondola he'd been offering one night, not a whole month of them... Alarm bells sounded at the intimacy of that. It was all impossible. 'It's not that simple. I can't just click my fingers and walk out of my life.'

His nostrils flared; it was obvious Ares Lykaios was not used to hearing the word no. She'd expected him to kiss her in an attempt to persuade her, or to throw money at her, or maybe even to remind her of the blackmail angle. Instead, he addressed the realities of making this work.

'I do a lot of work from here. I have office space to spare, with all the latest facilities and technology, excellent Wi-Fi, and if you're worried about how you'll manage Danica and whatever work you cannot pass off to someone else then we can work around that.' He paused a moment, lost in thought. 'Xanthia told me of a girl in the village who babysits. She can come and help during the days—so long as you agree to step in if there's a problem—so that you have time to yourself. Deal?'

She wanted to say no, just to thwart him, because he was moving the pieces of her life so effortlessly, showing such control and intuition.

But that ribbon around her chest was being tugged again, drawing her to him, showing her a glimpse of a more impulsive life. Weren't Amy and Clare always telling her to follow her instincts more? To listen to her gut? Well, both her instincts and gut were telling her to jump first, look later. They'd been telling her the same thing all night. And now Ares was making it easy for her to do just that.

'What is the expression about having cake and eating it as well?'

She lifted a hand to his chest, tempted beyond words. 'To have one's cake and eat it too,' she supplied, distracted.

'Exactly. Isn't this a way to do that?'

She sighed. 'It's...complicated.' The kiss they'd shared on the gondola felt like a lifetime ago—as though it had happened to a wholly different person. She couldn't believe how free she'd felt then!

'Why?'

Embarrassment rolled through her. She dropped her gaze, unable to look directly at him. 'I'm not someone who just casually…gets involved in relationships.'

He was quiet and, despite the fact they'd only known each other a short time, she knew exactly how he'd be looking at her, appraising her, trying to understand what she wasn't saying. Nerves flew like butterflies inside her belly.

'I mean, I never have before.'

She risked a glance at him; he was frowning.

'Been in a relationship?' he prompted. 'Let me re-assure you, Beatrice, I'm not offering anything seri-ous. This would be a strictly short-term arrangement.'

Her lips twisted in a half-smile. 'I don't mean that. I mean… I've never…' But she couldn't finish the sen-tence. She was twenty-nine and had never had sex. That didn't usually bother Bea, but now she found it morti-fying to confess.

'What is it?' he pressed. 'Are you trying to tell me you're a virgin or something?'

Her stomach swooped but she knew there was no sugar-coating it. Tilting her chin defiantly, she forced her eyes to meet his. 'Yes. That's exactly what I'm tell-ing you. I'm a twenty-nine-year-old virgin. Are you sure you still want to make sex a part of what you're offering?'

CHAPTER SEVEN

ALL THE AIR evacuated his lungs at once. He felt as though her words were rattling through his ears like a freight train on a looped track. It didn't make sense.

'You said you're twenty-nine.'

She fidgeted her hands at her sides, not meeting his eyes.

'And prior to taking up your role at the London Connection you were a senior partner in a law firm?'

'A top tier firm,' she confirmed, in that habit she had of babbling a little when she was nervous.

He nodded anyway, taking the titbit of information and filing it away.

'You are an intelligent, beautiful and kind woman. Twenty-nine years old. And yet you've never slept with a man?'

Her cheeks were bright pink and it was an unfortunate consequence of the situation that he found that mesmerising. His desire increased rather than doing what he wanted—and abating completely at her pronouncement.

But the way they'd kissed on the boat, the way her

body had moved over his, her hips pushing down on his masculine strength, showing with her body how much she needed him... 'So you've never had sex with a man,' he said with narrowed eyes. 'But you've obviously had some experience with other elements of lovemaking.'

Her throat moved in a delicate knot as she swallowed. 'You want my dating résumé now?'

'I think I'm entitled to some explanation.' It wasn't exactly the truth—he didn't feel entitled to anything, but he *wanted* an explanation and he hoped she'd give one.

Her eyes lifted to his, her mouth parting on a small sigh before she bit down on her lower lip. 'It's not a big deal.'

'I beg to differ.'

Hurt washed over her features; he regretted the words instantly. Hell, he was out of his comfort zone by about a thousand feet.

'I didn't intentionally mislead you. I didn't go to Venice expecting anything to happen between us. It was just work for me, nothing more. The gondola ride...' Her eyes assumed a faraway look as she tried to draw in breath. His gut rolled with a desire to kiss her. He stood his ground, his body like stone. He couldn't— wouldn't—give in to his instincts now. Not until he understood exactly what he was dealing with. A reformed nun? A runaway cult member? The idea of a twenty-nine-year-old virgin in this day and age beggared belief.

'The gondola ride was a total surprise. Put it down to the magic of the moonlight or something.' She laughed uneasily, awkwardly. 'And, as you know, coming back here wasn't on my agenda. You kidnapped me, remember?'

He remembered every detail of the evening they'd shared, and he knew this part would be forged in his memory banks in particularly vivid detail. 'Was your intention to save yourself for marriage?'

Her face scrunched up in a visceral reaction to that statement, a reaction he would have found amusing under any other circumstances. 'Don't be absurd. I'm never getting married.'

'That makes two of us. So what then?'

She closed her eyes, tilting her head towards the ceiling at the same time. 'Do we have to talk about this?'

'Help me understand and then I'll let it go.'

He had no real right to make demands of her, and yet Ares knew himself well enough to know he wouldn't rest until he understood. He liked things to make sense and this, quite simply, didn't.

'Is it really that big a deal? I just never met anyone I wanted to have sex with, that's all.'

'You didn't go through puberty?' he asked sceptically. 'It's my experience that at a certain point in everyone's lives hormones take control.'

She spun away from him and his fingers tensed with the desire to reach out and grab her, to turn her back to him, to pull her against his chest and listen to the rest of her explanation with her breasts crushed to him, her breath warming his throat. He ignored those instincts, aware that they were part of what had got them here in the first place.

'I was studying my backside off at an all girls school,' she said stiffly, sounding ever so prim. 'I didn't have time for boys.'

Despite himself, he smiled. He could imagine her saying exactly that to any friends who'd tried to lead her astray at the time. 'At university then?'

'Same deal, Ares. I studied. All the time. Some people seemed to be there to socialise, but not me. I worked hard and in any spare time I did have, I was helping Priti with the baby. I graduated with a first, and was offered a graduate role to start that summer.'

'And you didn't date that whole time?'

Her eyes sparked with something when they met his. 'I wasn't *interested* in dating. I wasn't interested in men. I wasn't interested in being lied to, told I was the love of someone's life just so they could get me into bed. I've seen it happen enough times to my friends to know that's the drill. I saw the way heartbreak torpedoed their lives and chose to avoid that for myself. Men, frankly, suck.'

Her words whirled around him. It was a speech laced with bravado, but he heard the hurt that underscored it. 'Heartbreak and sex don't have to go hand in hand. I'm sorry you've missed out on something so wonderful for so many years, simply because you were afraid.'

'I'm not afraid,' she rejected, so quickly it was obvious she hadn't given it a moment's thought.

For Ares, it was all he needed to push home his advantage. He hadn't realised he'd been laying the pieces of a trap—he'd played to win without even intending to—and now it was set.

'If that is true, you'll consider my proposition more seriously.'

Her eyes widened; he could feel her temptation.

'I will not break your heart, Bea, because I don't want it. I will not make you promises, I will not lie to you. I'm offering only sex.' His lips twisted with a hint of mockery. 'Nothing more complicated than that.'

He could feel her wavering, her certainties eroding, but it was too soon to celebrate. Too soon to rejoice in the fact that he would make her his. A heady rush of adrenaline at the prospect of being her first lover flooded his veins, but it wasn't time to act on it yet. She was staring at him appraisingly, a battle clearly being waged inside her mind.

'I think it would be foolish to stay here,' she said stiffly, so whatever jubilation he'd been feeling a moment earlier evaporated. But Ares Lykaios intended to win and there were two objectives for him that evening.

'Oh, make no mistake about it, you're staying here, Beatrice. At least you are if you value my business at the London Connection.'

He knew it was beneath him, but desperation to find someone who could help with Danica forced his hand there.

'I don't believe you,' she whispered. 'One minute you're asking me to make love to you and the next you're blackmailing me?'

'Not to sleep with me. Only to look after Danica,' he clarified, as though that made it any better. Since when had he become someone who stooped to this level? The answer was simple. On the streets of Athens, broke and starving, he'd done things as a teenager he knew to be reprehensible. Things that were against his strict moral code, all to ensure Matthaios's survival. He'd stolen food from grocery stores—not a lot, just enough to survive, but it had offended every cell in his body to do it. He'd hated that their impoverished state had required it of him. On one occasion he'd even stolen money from a tourist. A ten-euro note had been sticking out of her pocket, so close to falling. He'd walked behind her, waiting for it to drop and, when it hadn't, he'd brushed past her and taken it, aware that the money could make all the difference to Matt. He'd done what he'd needed to protect his brother, and now he was doing what he needed to protect Danica.

He didn't have to like himself for it though.

'Just to be stranded in this luxurious fortress for a whole month?'

He ground his teeth together. 'Think of it as an assignment.'

'I'm a lawyer. I don't get "assignments".'

'You're also a senior member of the London Connection, aren't you?'

'Stop banging me over the head with that,' she demanded haughtily. 'You don't need to keep reminding me of your importance to the company, and I'm well aware of the company's importance to me.' Her gaze clashed with his, cold anger stirring in their depths. 'But if you knew me, Ares, if you'd listened to anything I've said tonight, you would have known how unnecessary it was to go to such crude, bullying means to achieve your ends.'

He felt as though a boulder was pressing down on his chest, but didn't visibly react to her condemnation.

'I told you how I put my whole life on hold to help

Priti with her baby. Tonight, at the ball, I spent an hour with a little girl I didn't know just because I felt sorry for her. You could have pleaded with me on Danica's behalf and won me over. You didn't need to show yourself to be such a callous bastard.'

She sniffed, a sound of anger not sadness.

Provoked into responding with total honesty, he spoke unapologetically. 'I had to be sure of your cooperation. I could have played on your sympathy, certainly, but then you might have said no. In my experience, people are always motivated by money.'

She laughed dismissively. 'It's not *money* that's motivating me, you idiot. It's basic human decency, and love. Love for Clare and Amy and the business they've built up. Love for the clients they take care of with every breath in their bodies.' She pushed her hands onto her hips, looking at him as though he were scum. 'Even *you*,' she said witheringly. 'To think, Clare works her butt off for you and this is how you behave!'

Strange that earlier that very same day she'd gasped any time she said anything approaching an insult, apologising profusely. There was no sign of apology in her face now, just scathing condemnation.

It stirred an ache in his gut he'd never felt before.

'I take it that means you'll stay?'

Her eyes swept shut, her features taut and skin pale. 'Obviously.' The word was seething with disgust. He felt every measure of it in the core of his being.

'But as for sleeping with you,' she said coldly, moving towards him, pressing a finger to his chest. 'That's something I no longer have any interest in doing.'

It was a split-second decision. No, there was no decision-making about it. He acted purely on instinct, the same instinct that had seen him steal out of desperation as a starving teenager—he wasn't proud of it; it showed his darker side—roared to life now. He took hold of her finger, moving her hand to their sides, his eyes flashing with intention before he acted, his mouth claiming hers. Not like on the gondola—this wasn't a kiss of gentle, moonlit exploration, with waves splashing at their side. This was a kiss of desperate anger, a kiss of dominance, a kiss designed to entreat submission. Other than his hand holding her finger, he didn't touch her anywhere else. His mouth ravaged hers and she moaned, her body swaying forward, her abdomen pressing to his arousal. She made a low, keening noise as he grew harder against her, a whimper, and then a plea in his mouth.

How easy it would have been to take it further, to undress her and show her the full extent of her dishonesty. But Ares knew his limits, and he'd already stretched them well beyond an acceptable level. He broke his mouth free, staring down at her with darkly glittering eyes.

'You can lie to yourself all you want, Beatrice. Tell yourself you do not want to sleep with me, if you like. But don't lie to me, or I will take great pleasure in showing you the truth.' He stalked across the room, picking up the airphone and speaking a few words into it. He had his back to her—time he desperately needed to cool his temper and put a halt to the raging blood in his body. When he turned to face her, shame washed over him.

She was shaking like a leaf, so pale and fragile-looking. Regret chewed through him, but he refused to show any form of weakness. 'A member of staff is on their way to show you to your room. Goodnight, Beatrice.'

She wanted to strangle him. She wanted to put her hands around his throat and strangle him for what he'd done, but at the same time her anger was really all directed at herself. Her stupidity in kissing him back, in immediately begging him to make love to her. The way she'd pleaded with him, over and over, his name moving from her mouth to his, begging him for so much more than a kiss, wanting satisfaction and fulfilment as she never had before.

He'd been right about hormones. That was all this was. Some kind of pre-programmed biological response. Her oestrogen responding to his testosterone, causing a hurricane of desire she'd been unable to ignore.

All night she lay in the luxurious bed, staring at the ceiling, trying to work out if he'd carry out his threat if she were to leave. He was hugely important to the London Connection but it wasn't a one-way street. They were important to him too. He wasn't a man to suffer fools so, without knowing the details of previous PR campaigns and the ongoing management they did for his various business interests, she had to believe Clare was doing an excellent job for him. Surely he wouldn't rip his business away simply because she'd said no to helping him with a baby—a job for which, despite what he might think, she was manifestly unsuited.

Except, at the same time, Bea had to acknowledge

there was a risk. Although the London Connection was fast gaining recognition for its client management, there were other firms out there that had been established for much longer, that had more resources, bigger teams, larger reach. How many of the London Connection's clients had come across to them simply because they had someone like Ares Lykaios on their books?

It wasn't just about losing Ares's business then, but about losing the prestige that came from his association with them. Beatrice couldn't be responsible for that, and yet she was sorely tempted to roll the dice and see what happened. Despite his words, there was a part of her that suspected he was bluffing. She couldn't say why, but she had an undeniable faith in his inherent goodness and fairness—it was incompatible with his threat, and yet she felt almost certain that if she were to tell him she was leaving his home—come what may—he'd let her go, and continue working with Clare regardless.

But being almost certain wasn't good enough.

She prevaricated all night, veering from one opinion to the other. She tossed and turned and, somewhere in the early hours of the morning, before the sun had started its ascent into the night sky over Greece's Argolic Gulf, she gave up on trying to sleep and pushed out of bed. Her ballgown was where she'd left it—hardly suitable attire, but for lack of other options…

She had a quick shower and as she reached for a towel she saw that some clothes had been left folded on the cupboard beside the linen. The trousers were a size too big; she had to knot them at the waist to keep them from falling down, but the shirt—long-sleeved and a pale yellow in colour—was a perfect fit. She finger-combed her hair and rubbed a scented moisturiser over her face, regretting that sleep deprivation had left two brown smudges beneath her eyes, then defiantly reminding herself she didn't care.

She moved through the house, intending to hunt down a coffee, but a noise stopped her. Crying.

Baby crying.

Her feet moved towards the sound quickly and silently, piecing together the route to Danica's room. It wasn't easy. The house was huge and she'd been turned around by everything that had happened after she'd put Danica to bed. The crying grew louder though, leading her there, and she pushed the door inwards without hesitation, without a pause for what she might find on the other side.

It certainly wasn't this.

Ares stood dressed in only a low-slung towel, his chest bare, his hair damp, the crying infant in his arms. A lamp had been turned on near the bed, casting them both in a warm glow.

Bea's heart thumped painfully at the sight. He turned to look at her, his dark eyes defensive and then utterly bleak.

The baby howled. Bea held her ground, unable to move.

'Beatrice…' His voice was thick, groggy. 'Please… stay. We need your help.'

CHAPTER EIGHT

By LUNCHTIME HER HEAD was swimming.

Leave a baby to cry it out. Never leave a baby crying longer than a minute. Leave them to cry but stay in the room so they can see you at all times. Put toys above the bed to distract them and comfort them. Never over-stimulate a baby at bedtime: remove all toys from their line of sight.

So much contradictory advice, all from reputable-seeming parenting authorities, none of them particularly good at agreeing about how to soothe an unsettled baby.

'And you've definitely ruled out medical factors?' she asked, tapping her pen against the thick pile of pages she'd printed off the internet. Going back to her law school roots, she'd spent Danica's fitful daytime naps with a highlighter and notepad, intending to distil what she'd presumed would be a sort of parenting manual onto paper—a guide for both of them to ease Danica into a better routine.

'Cassandra had her checked over by several paediatricians,' he said darkly. 'None could find anything wrong with her.'

'Well, that's good,' Bea said, returning her attention to the pages because it was preferable to looking at Ares. She was still angry with him, she reminded herself, even when the image of him shirtless and comforting Danica was now imprinted on her eyeballs. 'With Nikki, it was just about routine,' Bea murmured thoughtfully. 'If we missed her naptime by even ten minutes, she'd be a nightmare for days. It was hard because Priti and I were both trying to study, but we ran the house like clockwork. It meant we could have a semblance of a normal life,' Bea concluded. 'I wonder if Danica is the same?'

Ares's only response was to lift—by a degree of millimetres—his shoulders.

Bea compressed her lips. 'Did Danica's nanny keep to a tight schedule?' she prompted.

Something flickered in Ares's face. 'I don't know.'

'Well, were her daytime naps all at roughly the same time? What about bedtime?'

'I am not someone who sticks to a strict routine,' he said eventually. 'The reason I hired a nanny who was so highly regarded was because I'm often away from home. Xanthia would be better placed to answer any questions about that.'

Bea shouldn't have been surprised. She tried to keep the judgement from her expression but unfortunately his remark hit way too close to home. How familiar that was to her! The notion of an adoptive parent outsourcing the parenting and consoling themselves with the fact that they'd hired 'the best'. Ares wasn't Danica's adoptive father but he was her uncle, and he was—for the moment—her closest family.

Ice chilled her heart as her own experience of familial rejection spiked through her, paining her all over again.

'I'll speak to Xanthia then.' She scraped her chair back, walking towards the door with a spine that was ramrod-straight. Unusually for Bea, she had the strangest sense she might cry.

'Wait.' His voice was commanding and insistent. Oh, how she'd have loved to ignore it! But that would be petulant and childish, and she refused to indulge either emotion.

She half turned to face him, her neck swan-like, her brown hair piled onto her head in a loose bun.

'What time will you put her to bed tonight?'

Bea had drawn up a schedule which seemed to contain a lot of overlap from the various parenting sites and books. 'Six-thirty. Why?'

'Once she is asleep, we'll go to Athens.'

She gave up on the half-turn and spun back to face him completely. 'What for?'

'You're here for a month. You'll need more to wear than a ballgown and Xanthia's husband's clothes.'

Bea looked down at the misshapen outfit with a raised brow. 'Really? I had wondered...'

'Meet me on the roof at seven.'

Bea pursed her lips, jolted back to the present. 'I can't do that.'

A scowl darkened his face.

'I don't know if she'll go to sleep straight away, and

FREE BOOKS GIVEAWAY

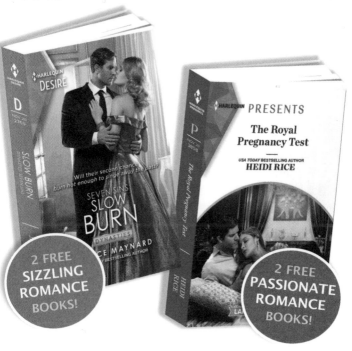

2 FREE SIZZLING ROMANCE BOOKS!

2 FREE PASSIONATE ROMANCE BOOKS!

GET UP TO FOUR FREE BOOKS & TWO FREE GIFTS WORTH OVER $20!

We pay for everything!

Complete the survey below and return it today to receive up to 4 FREE BOOKS and FREE GIFTS guaranteed!

FREE BOOKS GIVEAWAY
Reader Survey

1

Do you prefer stories with happy endings?

◯ YES   ◯ NO

2

Do you share your favorite books with friends?

◯ YES   ◯ NO

3

Do you often choose to read instead of watching TV?

◯ YES   ◯ NO

YES! Please send me my Free Rewards, consisting of **2 Free Books** from each series I select and **Free Mystery Gifts**. I understand that I am under no obligation to buy anything, as explained on the back of this card.

❏ **Harlequin Desire®** (225/326 HDL GQ4U)
❏ **Harlequin Presents® Larger-Print** (176/376 HDL GQ4U)
❏ **Try Both** (225/326 & 176/376 HDL GQ46)

FIRST NAME   LAST NAME

ADDRESS

APT.#   CITY

STATE/PROV.   ZIP/POSTAL CODE

EMAIL ❏   Please check this box if you would like to receive newsletters and promotional emails from Harlequin Enterprises ULC and its affiliates. You can unsubscribe anytime.

if she doesn't I'm not going to leave her to have another exhausting and traumatic screaming episode. It's not fair to Xanthia either.'

Tension arced between them, an argument in their eyes, and then finally he relented—after all, he could afford to lose the battle. He'd already won the war. 'I'll be waiting. Come up when you are ready.'

Bea should have been relieved that Danica went to sleep so easily. Surely that was a good sign that something about the routine she'd implemented was working? In the end, she'd followed her instincts. An early dinner, a warm, lightly fragranced bath, a calm book-reading in an almost dark room, followed by a bottle with Bea singing softly as Danica fed, a quiet cuddle and burp and then into bed. Bea kept her hand on Danica's chest lightly, as she'd done the night before, watching as the baby's beautiful blue eyes grew heavy and finally dropped closed, her breathing rhythmic as sleep swallowed her.

Xanthia was hovering on the other side of the door, her face lined with worry.

'She's asleep,' Bea whispered.

Xanthia's look of shock brought a smile to Bea's face. 'Already? But…how? It isn't possible!'

'She was tired, I think,' Bea said with a shrug. 'I've switched the monitor on. You'll keep an eye on her?'

'Of course, of course.' Xanthia was glowing. She looked as though she wanted to hug Bea. Instead, she clapped her hands together. 'Peace, at last! I have been so sad for the little girl—so much heartbreak and no one—' Xanthia cut herself off abruptly. 'I'm glad she has you.'

Strangely, so was Bea. Despite the fact it had only been one day, so much had happened that her London life already felt strangely distant. Almost as though she was looking at it through a sort of screen.

'Ares asked me to remind you he's waiting,' Xanthia added belatedly, as though just remembering the reason for being stationed outside Danica's door.

'Like I could forget,' Bea muttered. 'Please call if anything happens with the baby. I don't want her to be upset like she was last night.'

Xanthia nodded. 'Tomorrow morning, Ellen will come. A girl I know from the village. She has two younger brothers and three younger sisters, all of whom she helped raise. You'll like her.'

It had only been hours since she'd last seen him, but Bea still felt a jolt of something like awe at the sight of Ares Lykaios when she pushed open the door to the rooftop helipad some ten minutes later. He wore a suit that must have been made for his body, the darkest navy blue with a crisp white shirt open at the throat. He was designer, delicious and dangerous. Far too handsome for any one man.

Butterflies burst through Bea's belly and her legs were unsteady as she walked towards the gleaming black helicopter. As she approached, he lifted the aviator-style sunglasses from his eyes, hooking them in the top of his shirt and pinning her with a gaze that hollowed out what was left of her tummy.

'She's asleep?'

Bea nodded. She wanted to stay cross with him, to remember that he was palming off the care of his infant niece to a virtual stranger, and that he'd blackmailed her into being here, but at the same time images of him in just a towel, comforting Danica in the small hours of the morning, showed that to be a lie. He did love the baby, and he was doing what he could to care for her. He simply felt bewildered by the enormity of being thrust into the role of parenthood out of nowhere. Relenting, she offered him a cool half-smile. 'She seemed tired. Hopefully she'll sleep well.'

His relief was obvious. 'Thank you.'

And because she'd heard the helplessness in his voice that morning, when it had been just the two of them in Danica's nursery, she understood the depths of his gratitude.

'You're welcome.'

The air between them seemed to spark with awareness, or perhaps that was all coming from Bea. Close to Ares, alone on the rooftop, she wanted more than anything to feel the strength of his body close to hers once more, to lift her face to his and have him kiss her as though that were the most normal and natural thing in the world. And maybe it was—for other people. But not for Bea. She'd never wanted a relationship with a man, and even the kind of relationship he had suggested seemed fraught with danger.

Dragging her eyes away from his with determination, she realised they weren't in fact alone. A man in dark trousers and a pale shirt opened the door to the helicopter, smiling at Bea in an invitation for her to step inside. She took the same seat she'd occupied the night before, presuming Ares would do the same, but before he sat down he hovered over her, reaching for the straps of her seatbelt and fastening it into place, just as he'd done on the plane. Her breath held, her gaze was drawn to his face as if by magnetic force. She couldn't look away.

He pulled the seatbelt tight, his fingers lingering at her hip as he lifted his attention to her face and she had to bite back a moan. Awareness crashed through her like a tidal wave, a desire she'd never known before pressing bright sparks of light into her eyes.

His gaze roamed lower, landing on her lips, so she remembered every single sensation of having him kiss her the night before, the way he'd plundered her mouth with his, proving a point. And he had proved that point—she wanted to sleep with him, no matter what she'd thrown at him in the anger of their fight.

Desire stormed through her blood; she was helpless to fight it.

She surrendered a part of herself in that moment, acknowledging how much she wanted him. She was taken back to the way she'd felt on the gondola, when she'd been tempted to throw all caution to the wind and experience, for the first time in her life, what sex was all about.

'Ares—'

His name on her lips was a plea, drawn from deep within her.

And he understood. She saw it on his face that he

knew how she felt, and what she wanted. So it made absolutely no sense when he stepped back, taking the seat across from her, his expression neutral as he buckled his own belt in place.

Her cheeks felt as though they'd caught fire. She stared at him in disbelief, then blinked, turning her attention to the window. Uncertainty and need were looping through her. She felt completely out of her depth, an experience Bea had always hated.

Before she could contemplate pulling the pin on the whole idea of a shopping trip in Athens, the helicopter's blades began to whirl, the engine noise cutting out any possibility of conversation as the craft lifted up into the sky.

For a moment the view distracted her. The night before it had been pitch-black, and she'd spent the entire day enveloped in baby-related research. For the first time, as the helicopter took the trajectory of an eagle over the coastline, Bea realised how stunningly beautiful it was. The sun had not yet set but was on its way, painting the sky a dramatic palette of fiery oranges and pinks; the ocean below them was a deep turquoise, enhanced by the dusk light. She could see how sparsely populated the coastline was too, each house spaced several miles apart, each luxurious and modern, though Ares's most of all.

'Champagne?' The throaty-voiced offer had her turning to face him. A recognisable label on a piccolo bottle was being held towards her. She stared at it a moment before nodding, watching as he curled his palm around the cork and lifted it, the sound muted by his hand's tight grip. He placed a straw in the top, handing it across to Bea, and she took it gratefully.

'How long have you lived here?' she asked, simply to fill the silence—a silence that was throbbing with a drugging awareness.

'I bought the house ten years ago.' His lips twisted in a way that suggested to Bea he was concealing something.

'For any particular reason?' she asked.

'I liked it.'

She nodded thoughtfully. 'You look as though there's more to it than that.'

Surprise briefly flashed in his features and he was quiet for a moment, thinking, before he shifted his head once. 'When I was a boy I used to live just over there.' He pointed across the glittering bay to a small town on the water's edge. Unlike the sparsely populated coastal region where Ares's mansion stood, this village looked full to the brim, tightly packed houses jostling for space. 'My grandfather was a fisherman, and I'd go out with him sometimes. There were barely any houses here then. Two or three enormous sprawling homes that— to my eyes—looked like palaces.'

Bea sipped her champagne, listening intently.

'When I made my first billion American dollars I bought one of these homes.'

Bea gaped. 'Your first billion?' She shook her head a little ruefully. 'Exactly how many billions do you have?' She grimaced, regretting the forthright question immediately. 'Don't answer that. I shouldn't have asked.'

He flexed a brow. 'It's a matter of public record. I have no issue with you knowing.'

'Oh.'

'Current estimates put my wealth around the hundred-billion-dollar mark. It fluctuates a little, depending on international markets and world events.'

Bea blinked. 'I can't even imagine what that's like.'

A muscle jerked in his jaw. 'The thing about money is that once you have enough to feed yourself and your family, buy a secure home, a warm bed, it doesn't really change that much. There's not a huge difference between ten thousand dollars and ten billion, to my mind.'

Having lived through homelessness and poverty, Bea supposed he was uniquely placed to comment on that.

'You must have felt pretty damned good walking in that door for the first time though,' she said, nodding back towards his home, now a distant speck far beneath them.

'I felt better when I bought our first home, actually,' he said quietly.

'Our?'

'My brother, Matthaios, and mine. He was still at school. Back then I'd amassed what I thought was a fortune—spare change now, really, but to me, at the time, it was a king's ransom. Being able to buy an apartment outright, to know that, whatever happened, Matthaios would have somewhere safe to live—that was the best feeling I've ever known. This was enjoyable, but nothing will ever compare to that.'

'He's your younger brother?'

He nodded but his demeanour shifted, so that he seemed closed off and distant. 'He's two years younger.'

'You're close?'

A terse nod.

'You said he's sick?'

Ares's eyes flashed to hers, dark emotions tumbling through their depths. 'Yes.'

'I'm sorry. Is it serious?'

'It's a…lifelong condition.'

She frowned, sympathy tugging at her heart-strings.

He sighed heavily. 'My mother was a drug addict. My brother inherited her…tendencies. I should have re-alised sooner what was happening.' Self-directed anger thickened his voice. 'As teenagers, we had no money—he couldn't drink or do drugs; it simply wasn't an op-tion. But, once things improved for us financially, he found it easy to procure whatever the hell he wanted.'

Bea's heart tightened.

'I worked a lot. I didn't see what was right in front of me, despite having witnessed my mother's addiction play out for years. I should have known he was losing himself to drugs, alcohol—whatever he could get his hands on.'

She shook her head to dispel the blame Ares was laying at his own feet. 'You were working so you could support him,' she reminded Ares gently.

'That's no excuse. I should have realised.'

The helicopter changed direction, so that the ocean gave way to verdant land far below.

'By the time I saw what was happening, he was so far gone. It took years to convince him to go to rehab, and in the end I had to let him hit rock-bottom before he finally got there. You cannot imagine what that was like, Beatrice. Watching him self-destruct, knowing there was only so much I could do.'

Her throat shifted as she swallowed. Strangely, he didn't mind the sympathy on her face now.

'I could only keep him safe,' Ares admitted gruffly. 'I hired security to guard his house—and him—so that at least he was watched.' He shook his head angrily. 'They called me one morning when he wouldn't wake up. He'd come this close to an overdose.' He pinched his finger and thumb together.

'That's horrible,' she whispered.

He nodded. 'He spent two nights in hospital and then he chose to go to rehab. He begged me for help. I've never been gladder than I was in that moment.' He grimaced, because that happiness hadn't lasted long. As so often in life, a downfall had already begun to approach. 'He got sober, and turned his life around. He started an investment firm which did incredibly well, then met Ingrid and fell in love.' Ares's expression had assumed a faraway look and Bea knew that, though he was speaking aloud, he was really recounting the facts to himself, going over them as if he could make better sense of them somehow. 'Their wedding day was one of the happiest of my life. To know how far he'd come, to see the hope on his face, the love in his eyes… I felt… such immense relief, as though finally everything was going to be okay.'

'And then Ingrid died,' Bea said softly.

He lifted his eyes to her face, torment in his features.

'Yes. Ingrid died and my brother was left with a black hole of grief and a tiny, dependent child. I should have done more. I should have—'

Bea made a frustrated sound and leaned as far forward as she could, putting a hand on his thigh to draw his attention fully. 'You can't blame yourself for this.'

'Can't I?' he asked quietly, his voice still ringing with self-condemnation. 'I'd seen what he'd been through before. I'd seen my mother grapple with her demons for years. I knew how desperately he needed to blot out the pain. I should have done more to help him.'

'What more could you have done?' she asked logically.

Ares stared at her.

'He's a grown man. Your job isn't to live Matthaios's life for him, Ares. It sounds to me like you've done the best you can for your brother all your life, and you're still doing that now.'

'You don't understand. I should have seen what was coming. I should have predicted he'd turn back to drugs. I should have—'

'Kidnapped him to your mansion for all eternity?' she couldn't help teasing, despite the serious tenor of their conversation.

His eyes flared, showing surprise at her quip.

'You couldn't chain him up until his grief passed. And you couldn't watch him twenty-four hours a day. Did you support him, Ares? Did you call to check on him? Ask how he was, how the baby was?'

His face paled. 'I spent a month with him, after her death. Then I had dinner with him several times a week.

I hired security, as before, to keep them both safe. I hired nannies—he fired them. But still I thought he was doing well, given the circumstances. He seemed heartbroken but well, at the same time. I looked for signs of addiction. I checked his house when he was occupied with Danica, and I called at unusual times, wondering if I would detect something in his voice that spoke of drug use or alcohol abuse. I detected *nothing*. I missed the signs.'

'Or maybe he was holding it together and then something happened and he had a bad few nights. Or maybe he was just that good at hiding his behaviour from you…' She paused, frustrated that he couldn't see how much help and support he'd offered. 'But look at what you've done for him now. He's getting treatment and help, and you've stepped in to care for Danica, so that when he comes out his beautiful baby will be waiting for him. If you hadn't done that she would have ended up in foster care, Ares. Do you have any idea what that would have meant? It would have been far from guaranteed that Matthaios would be able to take Danica back when he was ready. You've given him a second chance to be a father—that's something to be proud of.'

His gaze shifted to her hand, still on his thigh, and he looked at it for so long that her fingers began to tingle and warm. She was about to retract it when his own hand came down on hers, keeping it right where it was.

'You were adopted.'

The statement shattered something inside her. A shame Bea worked hard to rationalise away burst through her at the unexpectedness of his words, a shame that came from knowing how unwanted she was: by her birth parents first, by her adoptive parents ultimately. A sour taste flooded her mouth and she went to pull her hand away again, but he held on tightly, his eyes loaded with warning when they met hers. Under his intense scrutiny her pulse began to go haywire.

'So?' Her voice shook with defiance, dredged from deep within her soul. She didn't need anyone to love her; what did it matter that she'd been rejected by all the people who were meant to love her most? She'd worked herself into the ground to build her career, and she had Amy and Clare.

'I just wondered if you're speaking from experience.'

Her breath evacuated her lungs on one huge whoosh. 'No.'

She pulled away then and he let her. Bea tried to ignore the coldness spreading inside, and the fear that he was seeing more of her than she wanted him to—more than she'd ever let anyone see. To the world, Bea was an in-control lawyer, intelligent, bright and driven. No one needed to know the gaping wounds that existed in her heart, the feeling that there must be something inherently wrong with her to have been rejected so consistently. Her secret fear—that no one would ever love her or want her enough—was just beneath the surface, though.

She wouldn't let Ares know how broken she was inside. For some reason he was the last person she wanted to see beyond her façade.

CHAPTER NINE

SHE WASN'T LIKE any woman he'd ever known. She'd shunned the high-end boutiques his chauffeur had brought them to, wrinkling her nose up at the clothes the assistants had suggested, repeatedly walking out empty-handed, despite his insistence that he wanted to furnish her with a wardrobe to get her through the month they'd agreed on.

Had they agreed? He couldn't precisely remember. The night before had gone as far from his expectations as possible, and yet somehow he had taken the fact that she was still here as tacit consent that she'd remain.

He'd wondered if she was just being contrary to spite him, but as they'd passed a department store she'd stopped walking and pressed a hand to his chest. 'Perfect. Wait here.'

He'd ignored her suggestion, following behind as Bea whipped through the chainstore's women's fashion offerings. She scooped up clothes as she went. A pair of jeans, a denim skirt, some shorts, several T-shirts in the same style and different colours, before turning around and pushing the selection into his arms.

'Hold these.' Her eyes challenged him. 'Do not follow me into the lingerie section, Ares. I mean it.'

Oh, how sorely tempted he was to do exactly that! But her innocence put him in an unusual position—torn between his desire for her and a need to tread gently, reminding himself that she wasn't like his usual lovers.

Oh, she was beautiful and smart, sophisticated and intelligent, but she was also a virgin, and for a man like Ares who'd only ever offered one part of him to the women he slept with—his body—surely that innocence made her off-limits? All the more so because he couldn't offer her more than a physical relationship. Sex. His temperature skyrocketed and in the middle of the department store his body grew hard, his arousal tight against the seam of his trousers so he lowered the bundle of clothes a little. What the hell was wrong with him? The fact she was a virgin should have been a huge red flag. He shouldn't be interested in being her first, but hell, he wanted her regardless.

He hovered on the edge of the section, determined not to look in her direction. Instead, he wandered, finding himself amongst Lycra swimsuits and picking several out simply to keep busy. The deep red bikini would complement Bea's complexion, but so too the cream with gold straps. He ignored the black one-piece even when he knew, somehow, that the bland, unflattering style was the one she would have gone for. He returned to the clothing section then, picking up a floral dress with a cinched-in waist and buttons down the front, adding it to the clothes she'd chosen, before Bea approached him, already carrying a plastic bag with the store's logo emblazoned on the front.

'Let's go pay for those,' she said, unable to meet his eyes.

His stomach clenched at her coyness. She'd bought the underwear already, rather than risk him seeing them? It was yet another reminder of how different she was to the kind of women he usually dated—women who would happily swan around semi-naked in silken lingerie.

He knew he shouldn't tease her, but he couldn't resist. 'Did you find what you were looking for?'

She nodded, reaching out for the clothes without looking, but he shook his head. 'I'll take care of it.'

'Then I'll go wait outside,' she said breathily, apparently desperate to escape.

He watched her make a beeline for the exit and then turned on his heel, heading back into the lingerie section. He had no doubt she'd chosen boring cotton panties and bras. That was fine. But Ares wanted to add something else to her wardrobe, something that she might wear and imagine him removing...

There was a meagre selection of sensual nightgowns in this family-friendly store, but he managed to find a slinky black negligee with lace detailing, and a matching pair of French lace panties. He whistled as he made his way to the checkout, unable to think of anything except Bea in sexy lingerie, against the sheets of his bed.

'We really should get back,' she said quietly, as much to herself as Ares. The truth was, she didn't want to return to his home just yet. Being in Athens with Ares, it was almost possible to forget what had happened the night before, the way he'd bullied her into staying with him, to help take care of Danica.

No, it wasn't that she'd forgotten. It was simply that the more time she spent with him, the more she understood him. She saw how motivated he was by his love for his brother, his desperate need to care for his family— and that included Danica. He'd move mountains to be sure the little girl was cared for, and last night Bea had represented the best chance for him to do that.

'We should eat,' he contradicted firmly, taking the bags from her hands and passing them to the waiting chauffeur. 'There is a nice French restaurant near here. Shall we see if they have duck à l'orange?'

His recollection of the small detail sparked something in her blood, something she found very difficult to suppress.

She wasn't used to anyone paying that much attention to her. Amy and Clare aside, and Priti when they were at university, Bea had never been important enough to anyone for them to care about the small things she said. It had been a throwaway comment, for goodness' sake!

But she wasn't important to Ares. That wasn't what this meant. He was just a control freak with an eye for detail. How else could he have achieved what he had in the business world?

'Danica...' she reminded him weakly.

'Xanthia would have called if there was a problem. I'm sure she's fast asleep.'

Bea bit down on her lip, tempted.

'A quick dinner, and then home,' he insisted, putting a hand in the small of her back, taking advantage of her prevarication.

'I suppose so.' And, despite the fact it was a suggestion of practicality, a burst of anticipation spread through her limbs, so she felt a smile crossing her face as they walked. It was dark now, the sky an inky black. The hand at the curve of her spine moved sideways, catching her hip and drawing her closer as though it were the most natural thing in the world. He held her close to his side, moulding her body to his, and she indulged a need for that closeness, lingering beside him, feeling the power of his steps as they moved through the cobbled streets of Athens.

'This is where you lived when you were a teenager?' she asked, partly to fill the silence and partly because she wanted to piece together everything there was to know about Ares.

She felt him tense and wondered if he wasn't going to answer. 'Yes. After my grandfather died we had nowhere to go.'

'Your mother?'

'She'd left us with him many years earlier. She disappeared; we didn't know how to contact her.'

'I'm sorry.'

He slowed down so she looked up at him, and their eyes clashed with a fierce strength of emotion that almost toppled Bea. She sucked in a gulp of air and turned her face forward once more, her skin prickling with goosebumps.

'We came here, thinking it would be easier to find

work. It wasn't. Hostels were often full, so more nights than not we were on the streets.'

Her heart was heavy, imagining the teenager he'd been then. 'You must have been terrified.'

'I was many things,' he said cryptically.

She tilted her face to his once more.

'The hardest part was the hunger. I'd never known anything like it. My grandfather didn't have much money but fish were plentiful, and he grew vegetables in pots. We ate well enough. When we came to Athens it was so hard. I will never forget trying to sleep through that dull, throbbing ache in my gut, knowing my little brother was feeling it ten times worse.'

Emotions throbbed in Bea's chest, sympathy chief amongst them.

'Having enough money to buy food became my primary concern. I used to watch people walk past in their expensive clothes and shoes, looking so happy and carefree. I promised myself, and Matthaios, that one day that would be us.'

His lips twisted in a dark grimace. 'Being carefree isn't something any amount of money can buy though.'

She jerked her head in agreement. 'There's no correlation between wealth and happiness,' she said softly.

'You have experience of this?' he prompted, leading them down a smaller alleyway. Buildings were tightly packed here, with bright flowerpots bursting with lavender and geraniums, some with small citrus trees, making the already narrow lane a tight squeeze, so he had to hold her even closer to his side.

'My adoptive parents had money,' she said quietly.

'But I don't know if I'd ever describe them as happy. My mother is…hard to please. In my experience, that's kind of the enemy to happiness.'

He nodded slowly, bringing them to a stop outside a brightly painted turquoise door. It had a glass panel and a moment later it was pulled inwards, so that any response Ares might have been poised to make was swallowed by the greeting of the waiter. He spoke in Greek, addressing Ares as an old friend, pulling the door open wider.

'You come here often?' Bea prompted, feeling self-conscious now in Xanthia's husband's clothes and wishing she'd taken the time to change into some of the items she'd chosen at the department store.

'From time to time,' he replied, gesturing to a table by a window. A candle was set in a round wine bottle, with long tendrils of wax showing that various others had melted in the same bottle top well before this one.

He held the chair out for her, and as she took her seat his hands brushed across her shoulders, sending little flames scurrying through her veins.

'Was she hard on you, when you were growing up?'

It took Bea a moment to realise he was talking about her mother again. She never liked talking about her childhood, but she especially resented its intrusion now. She pushed a bland smile to her lips, reaching for a menu instead of answering.

'What do you usually order here?'

His long, confident fingers reached over and removed the menu, replacing it on the tabletop. 'I always let the chef choose. Answer my question.'

She blinked at him. She shouldn't have been surprised by his demand. After all, this was the man who'd point-blank insisted she remain at his home even when she'd told him she wouldn't. Ares got what he wanted, and right now he wanted to know something about her.

She swallowed past the bundle of nerves in her throat, relieved when another waiter approached their table, asking if they'd like a drink.

She remembered enough Greek from that long-ago summer spent in the islands to respond in his native tongue, asking for a soft drink. Ares opted for a glass of red wine.

'You speak some Greek?'

'Just a little,' she said. 'I travelled around the islands for a few months, back when I was in school. I picked up a bit.'

'I didn't realise you'd been here before. Where did you go?'

She listed the islands, smiling as memories of that time swept through her. 'I could be completely myself here; I loved it. The people were so welcoming—no one knew anything about my parents or me. There were no god-awful British paparazzi following me, looking for an unflattering photo, trying to turn me into some kind of B-grade tabloid fodder.' She winced, too distracted to care that she'd revealed so much of herself.

He immediately pounced. 'Why would paparazzi chase you?'

She waved a hand through the air dismissively. 'My mum was a supermodel, my dad a rock star. Despite the fact he hasn't been on tour since I was a young girl, in

Britain he's still idolised, and Mum loves to "stay current", as she says. She has all the glossy mags do interviews with them every year; some come to the house for in-depth features. You know the kind of thing—"what life's like in the Jones family".' She rolled her eyes, wondering if the few sips of champagne she'd had in the helicopter had loosened her tongue so much, even when she suspected it was far more likely to be the effect of the man sitting opposite.

'Let me just say this…' She paused as the waiter appeared with their drinks, and so Ares could advise the waiter that they'd eat what the chef recommended.

'Do you have any allergies?' he asked Bea.

She shook her head.

Once they were alone again he reached across the table, putting his hand on hers. 'Go on.'

That simple gesture, as well as his prompting her to continue, warmed something that had been frozen in her chest for a very long time.

'Oh, just that what life looks like in the pages of those magazines is often a far cry from the truth.' A sense of disloyalty had her dropping her gaze. 'Or perhaps that's just being mean-spirited. I shouldn't have said it.'

'Is it true?'

Sparkling hazel eyes lifted to his. After a moment's hesitation, she nodded silently.

'Then you can say it.'

Nonetheless, perhaps sensing her reluctance to share further personal details, he moved the conversation to safer ground, asking about her studies instead, and her time as a senior partner, her career ambitions, and then her friendship with Amy and Clare, so, before Bea knew it, the dessert plates were being cleared and her stomach was full of the most delicious food she'd ever eaten.

'Oh, my goodness.' She stared at her watch with a look of panic. 'That wasn't a "quick meal"! We've been hours!'

'Yes,' he agreed, leaning back in his chair, completely confident and content. 'And while you were in the restroom earlier I checked in with Xanthia. Danica is still sleeping soundly. See? You are a magician.'

Relief and pride spread through Bea. 'I'm so glad. I hated seeing her as she was last night.'

'She has been like that most nights since she came to live with me.'

Bea tilted her head to the side a little. 'Babies are very intuitive,' she said thoughtfully. 'It's often believed that because they look helpless they are, when really they're capable of understanding so much more than we give them credit for.'

He waited for her to elaborate.

She chose her words with care. 'It sounds like Danica's life has already known no shortage of trauma and grief. The loss of her mother, her father's grief, and now his absence... It doesn't really surprise me that she's been struggling to settle.'

'So why were you able to calm her last night?'

Bea had her own theories on that, but she wasn't about to spout them to Ares. He hardly needed to know that Bea wondered if her own latent childhood traumas and grief had somehow spoken to Danica on some level, bonding them in a unique, unusual way, reassuring the little girl that she was in the company of someone who understood her pain.

'I don't know.' She shrugged. 'But I'm glad it worked.'

His laugh was unexpected. It spread like warm butter over her body. 'As am I.'

He ran his finger around the rim of his glass, his eyes probing hers in a way that sent shivers down her spine.

'I find it impossible to believe you've never dated before.'

The observation was completely unexpected and it roused her out of the heavenly state of relaxation she'd allowed herself to fall into. Sitting up straighter, she looked around.

'You must have been asked out?'

Bea bristled. 'I can't see how that matters.'

His smile was lightly mocking. 'Can't you?'

She looked down at her own drink, then his, mesmerised by the way his finger was moving.

She pursed her lips, searching for words. 'I'm twenty-nine. Of course I've been asked out.'

'So you've never said yes?'

She bit down on her lip, nodding warily.

'That makes no sense.'

'Apparently it takes a kidnap scenario to get me to go on a date,' she responded, only half joking.

Undeterred, he leaned forward, his legs brushing hers beneath the table. Her eyes widened. 'Haven't you ever wondered what it's like?'

'Dating?'

He shook his head slowly from side to side, not touching her, and yet heat spread through Bea's body as though his hands were on hers. 'No, *agápi mou*. Being made love to, slowly, gently, until you can barely breathe for how turned on you are.'

She gasped at the fever his words had incited.

'Or being made love to hard and fast because your lover cannot wait to make you theirs.'

Her lungs worked on overdrive.

'Have you never touched yourself, imagining your hands were those of a man you wanted? Touched yourself and wished it was your lover's mouth, worshipping you in your most sacred place?'

'Ares…' Again, his name was a plea on her lips. 'Please…' She didn't know if she was asking him to stop or begging him not to.

'I would like to show you what you're capable of feeling, *poulaki mou*,' he murmured. 'If only this were not so complicated.'

Oh, she wanted that too. She wanted it so badly she was terrified to admit her feelings. 'Why is it complicated?' she asked instead. 'I should have thought it's the most basic biological act.'

His smile was cynical. 'And yet you're a virgin.'

Her eyes dropped to the table.

'I do not sleep with virgins.'

She gasped. 'Is that a rule or something?'

'It might as well be.'

Disappointment speared her belly. She wanted to shake him, to tell him he was being silly. But then what?

Confusion, heat, need—all these feelings rushed through her like a live wire of electricity.

'Then...what...?'

When she risked a glance at him, he was appraising her silently.

She gathered her courage, forcing herself to speak her mind. 'Why are you flirting with me?'

His eyes were mocking, but was it directed at himself or her?

She waited, breath held, for his response, and yet she wasn't prepared for what was coming.

'Because I want you. Even though I know it's wrong, and that I can't offer you what you deserve, I look at you and feel as though I am fighting a losing battle.' Now his expression held a challenge, as though he were laying down a gauntlet. 'You've never had sex before and, despite what I just said, I find myself obsessing over being your first lover. I want to be the one who awakens you to the physical pleasures of intimacy. I have no doubt that's selfish of me, and yet here we are.'

Her breath wouldn't come easily. She stared at him in disbelief, her pulse racing, her mind blank. 'Ares...' But what could she say in response to that? He was offering her exactly what she wanted. She finally managed to suck in a deep breath, doing her best to think straight.

'I don't want more than sex.' She blurted the words out loudly and blushed to the roots of her hair, looking around to make sure that she hadn't been heard. 'Perhaps that's part of what's held me back from dating. The idea of a relationship is anathema to me. You don't need to worry I'll want more from you. Just…sex…is fine.' She cleared her throat. 'More than fine, in fact.'

What the hell was she doing? The water was up to her neck; she was about to drown. Or was she swimming? She couldn't tell. She knew only that it felt good and right to speak like this—two adults outlining a new set of rules, an agreement that would protect them both. There was comfort in the sanity of that when every other part of her felt disconnected from reality.

'It would change nothing between us.' There was wariness in his voice, but also the hard edge of control, as though he was on the brink of losing it.

'Fine by me.' A breathless agreement.

Their eyes met and it was like the signing of a contract. Without words, Ares stood, holding his hand out. Bea stared at it long and hard and then slid hers into his palm, fire zapping through her veins.

He didn't speak as they left the restaurant, but she answered him—and herself—nonetheless. 'I'm ready.'

CHAPTER TEN

HE'D TAKEN THE helicopter ride from Athens to Porto Heli thousands of times, but never quite like this. The tension in the helicopter could have been cut with a knife. She sat opposite him without talking, her hands fidgeting in her lap so her anxiety became all he could focus on. Not her anxiety so much as how he could alleviate it, show her that her body knew what it wanted and could be trusted to guide her. He knew that once they were home he could take charge, pleasuring her until all doubts fell from her mind.

There were no familiar landmarks beneath—it was too dark to see anything properly, but he knew—to the minute—the time it should take to arrive. He checked his watch, relief spreading through him when they reached single digits and then, finally, his home came into view. Her eyes were on him, watching, appraising, and anticipation spread through him. He ached to touch her, to feel her warm softness beneath his palm, her silky hair in his fingers, entangled in his grip, her beautiful body beneath his, welcoming him, losing herself to the heady rush of sensual euphoria.

The fact that he would be her first tightened his arousal to the point of pain. Now that he knew there was no risk of emotional entanglement, he could simply enjoy the pleasure of Beatrice Jones. The helicopter had barely touched down before he was moving, unclipping his own belt before attending to hers. Bea's fingers were shaking when he took her hand in his, but when she looked at him he didn't see what he'd expected to. There was no hesitation in her face, only the same blinding urgency that was exploding in his chest.

The night was cool and he held her close as they moved to the door, partly to keep her warm and partly because he was selfish and simply wanted to touch her, to feel her. Her body was slender but curved; he hungered to feel her in his hands. At the stairs, he dropped his arm, taking her hand in his as he led the way, pausing only briefly at the bottom, waiting for her to take the last step before he strode down the corridor, towards his bedroom.

Bea was right there with him. Until he opened the door and drew her through it, shutting them in his room, he didn't realise he'd been half terrified she'd change her mind. He turned to face her in the dimly lit space, just a lamp near the window casting the room in a gentle glow, and every rush of need that had been tormenting him since they'd left the restaurant burst through him now. His chest rocked with the torturous act of breathing, his body tense. He stared down at her and she looked up at him, and then he moved.

He'd kissed her twice before and this was like the second time, full of urgency, a kiss that overtook him with need, that seemed to happen almost without his control—something Ares would ordinarily despise. But anything that could bring his body to hers like this and have her dissolving against him in a soft, whimpering form of surrender had his approval. He took a step forward, pressing her against the back of the door, his tongue duelling with hers, demanding her supplication. Over and over she said his name, moaning it into his mouth as best she could, her hands pulling his shirt from his trousers, pushing at the buttons until her fingertips could touch bare flesh.

Her need to explore and touch was as real as his own. Despite her inexperience, she was guided by instincts and they were strong, so that if she hadn't told him she'd never been with a man he wouldn't have guessed it. Bea made a growling sound as she yanked at his shirt, separating it finally, removing it from his body as though she couldn't live another second without seeing him naked. He understood.

His hands completed the same task, removing the unsophisticated clothes she wore, stripping her down to her underwear and then dispensing with them so she was naked against him, her body warm and soft, just as he'd fantasised. Her hair was still up in a topknot; he pulled it loose as he kissed her, spilling her hair over her shoulders and down her back, before stepping back to admire her. The sound of their harsh breathing filled the bedroom, loud and demanding. He needed a moment though to commit her to his memory banks just as she was. Her cheeks pink, her chest too from his stubble, her pert breasts with peach nipples tautened by desire, her flat stomach and gently curved thighs.

He swore under his breath, holding out a hand. She put hers in it and he drew her to the bed, knowing he had to curb all his own selfish impulses—the desire to simply drive himself into her sweet sex and lose himself there, to take her hard and fast until they were both incandescent with pleasure. There'd be time for that—a month, in fact. A month to enjoy her sweetness and to teach her how great sex could be.

Tonight was about being gentle. Gradually introducing her to lovemaking without overwhelming her and, hell, without hurting her.

He scooped her up without warning, laying her down in the middle of the bed, kissing her as he moved his body over hers, still kissing as he extended an arm and lifted a condom from the bedside table. He discarded it near them on the bed—for later. First, he wanted to taste.

The sensation of his mouth on her breasts sent sharp arrows of pleasure-pain spiralling through Bea so she lifted her hips in a sudden, jerky movement. It was almost too much. Too intimate—too personal. He took one nipple between his teeth, rolling it there a moment before flicking it with his tongue, while his hand moved between her legs, brushing her femininity lightly at first, so she didn't know what to focus on, nor which feeling was more overwhelming. She knew only that she was coming apart at the seams in some vital, unmistakable way.

His hand between her legs was heaven-sent, but also not enough. She bucked her hips again, silently begging him for something she couldn't explain. He understood though; she felt him smile against her breast as he kissed his way downwards, his tongue swirling invisible circles around her belly button, over the plane of her stomach and low, teasing her hipbone before moving between her legs.

She groaned as his tongue touched her there, lightly at first and then with more intensity, more speed, more everything, delivering her towards a destination she'd never heard of, never even known about. She dug her nails into the bed first, then his shoulders, as her moans grew louder and louder and eventually she was tipping off the edge of the earth, pleasure swallowing her whole, changing her for ever.

But before she could recover she was dimly aware of the sound of foil and then his knee was parting her legs, his body over hers, his mouth kissing her softly as he pushed the tip of his arousal against her sex.

Despite the heavenly pleasure he'd already delivered, tension filled her. She whimpered, fear widening her eyes so she stared up at him for reassurance. His response was to speak in Greek, his words gentle and soft, words she didn't understand but which succeeded in reassuring her.

He wasn't gentle now. At least, not *so* gentle. He pushed into her, watching her the whole time as his arousal stretched parts of her previously untouched, his body possessing hers for the first time, breaking through an invisible barrier so that briefly she felt a sting of pain, a sharp, visceral response to his presence. It abated almost immediately, and she nodded, a silent encouragement to a question he hadn't asked.

It was then that he began to move. Then that Bea realised whatever pleasure she'd felt a moment ago, it was nothing to the overwhelming, all-consuming delight of this. His body mastering hers, his weight on top of her, the roughness of his chest hairs against her breasts, his hard erection deep inside her, being squeezed by muscles that were trembling in pleasure. Stars danced against the lids of her eyes; she was falling from heaven, or perhaps flying through it? She tilted her head back, capitulating to this madness completely, utterly lost and completely found all at once.

'How do you feel?'

It was a question with no answer. How could she describe how she felt in words? She turned her head to face him, her hooded eyes roaming his features with renewed speculation and interest. She felt a primal claim to him—as though he were hers in some vital, unchangeable way, and always would be.

Oh, it was a stupid way to feel. She recognised that almost immediately. No one person could belong to another and, even if they could, sex wasn't a gateway to possession. For someone like Ares, this had probably been a perfectly run-of-the-mill bout of sex. Just because the very parameters of Bea's world had been significantly redefined didn't mean it had meant anything to Ares.

He frowned, his finger lifting to trace her lips. She

sucked in a breath, the small act somehow seeming intimate despite what they'd just shared.

'Fine.' She cleared her throat. The word was banal and inaccurate. She felt so much better than fine. She felt shiny and new. She felt desirable and sensual. She felt wanted.

The realisation had her smile dropping, just by a fraction.

Careful, Bea.

She knew the inherent risks of that feeling. Being wanted was something she'd never experienced; it was a loss she'd had to accept in her life. She couldn't start looking to someone like Ares Lykaios to fill that vital void within her.

Sex was sex. Nothing more. They'd agreed on that.

The bath water was the perfect temperature and, as she sank into it, Bea acknowledged that she was a little sore. Parts of her body that had never been used made themselves known, so she winced a little.

He was watching, and a small grimace appeared on his own features in response.

'I'm fine,' she promised. And then, because he seemed genuinely worried, 'Better than fine, in fact.'

His smile was her reward. It shifted across his face, changing his features completely, so, for a moment, all she was capable of was staring. 'I'll be back.'

She was tempted to make a Terminator joke but he was gone too quickly. When Ares returned he was naked, holding two glasses filled with a pale amber liquid.

'Scotch?' She wrinkled her nose.

'You don't like it?'

'I've never tried it.'

'That seems to be the theme of the night,' he quipped, placing the glass on the edge of the bath before he stepped in, taking a seat opposite her. The tub was large—easily able to accommodate them both—yet their legs brushed and she was glad. The contact was a different sort of intimacy. She welcomed it and cherished it even as her own warnings swam through her mind. She knew she could balance the physical delight of his presence against the mental knowledge of his impermanence in her life.

Not just *his* impermanence. Everyone's. The unreliability of other people. Bea had sworn a long time ago that she'd never depend on another soul, certainly not for something as important as her happiness. She would enjoy this moment while knowing how fleeting it was. Convinced she could balance those beliefs, the germ of an idea flared in her belly.

'So, I've been thinking,' she murmured, reaching for the Scotch glass, her voice level despite the buzz of what they'd shared.

'Go on.'

His tone was cool, muted, and she hid her smile behind the glass.

'Perhaps I will stay here for a month.'

He tipped his head back and laughed, a deep noise that reached inside Bea and squeezed her tummy.

'I mean, not just because I really, really like what we just did,' she said with a lift of her shoulders.

'Of course not,' he murmured, mock serious. 'This would still be purely business.'

'Oh, absolutely. I might even have to call you Mr Lykaios from time to time,' she said, tilting her head to the side as she considered that. 'Or sir, if you'd prefer.'

He grinned, finishing his own Scotch before placing the glass on the edge of the bath and moving closer to her.

'As your self-appointed instructor in all things sexual, that does seem appropriate.'

'You mean there's more to learn?' she enquired with wide eyes.

'Oh, Beatrice, so much more. Where to start…?'

As always, he woke with a start, a sense of foreboding knotting in his gut that drew him immediately into consciousness. It didn't ease when he became aware of the warm, naked body at his side, her soft brown hair fanned across the pillow, stirring needs within him that should have been well and truly satiated by the night they'd shared.

On the streets of Athens he'd slept with one eye open, aware that danger could come at any point and that if it did it would be his responsibility to defend them both, to protect Matthaios. It was an alertness for danger that could only be eased in one way: control.

Ares didn't lose sleep about his business interests because he oversaw every single aspect of his empire. No matter was too small to escape his attention. In his personal life it was much the same.

Everything was on his terms, always.

The women he dated understood that—he made sure of it. Just as he had with Bea. He'd been crystal-clear.

Despite that, he felt a deep, dark worry that he might hurt her. He couldn't say why, but he had the strongest sense that there was something within Bea that needed protecting, a vulnerability she desperately tried to conceal, but which he nonetheless sensed.

He wouldn't hurt her.

They'd both acknowledged what this was, and he'd been open about the limitations of it. They'd even put an expiry date on her remaining with him. Surely that was some form of insurance?

Fighting a strong desire to wake her with the kind of kiss that would lead to so much more, he slid out of bed and dressed quickly, dragging on some low-slung jeans and a black shirt. If Danica woke he didn't want the crying to disturb Bea—she needed to sleep.

At the door, he took one last look at her. She was so beautiful and peaceful, so…trusting when she was asleep.

Despite the assurances he'd just given himself, the sense of foreboding was back, chewing at his gut. He pulled the door shut behind himself.

'Excuse me,' Bea apologised, stifling the fifth yawn in as many minutes.

Ellen's expression was sympathetic. 'The baby kept you awake last night?'

Heat suffused Bea's cheeks as she smiled awkwardly, looking away, infinitely preferring not to think about all the ways in which she'd been kept awake. Not by a baby, but by the sinfully sexy Ares Lykaios instead.

'Xanthia says you have a heap of experience with children.'

'I have lots of younger brothers and sisters,' the girl agreed, her round face dimpling as she smiled affectionately. 'And I have been hired as a babysitter since I was about nine years old,' she added.

'How old are you now?' Bea prompted.

'Twenty-one. I know I look younger,' Ellen laughed.

'Yes, you do,' Bea agreed, gesturing for Ellen to walk on ahead, into the lounge. Danica was set up in a playpen, lying on her tummy with a soft baby's ball in the palm of her hand.

Ellen made a little squealing sound of delight. 'Oh, she's so beautiful. May I pick her up?'

'Please,' Bea encouraged, interested to see how well Ellen handled Danica. The surge of protective instincts firing through Bea surprised her. As with the first night she'd held Danica, it was an almost maternal humming in her blood, a feeling that there was an invisible cord connecting the two of them, that she would fight to protect with her life.

Ellen spoke in Greek to the little girl, something that was wholly appropriate but which felt like a knife being plunged into Bea's heart. She felt excluded and unwanted. Old feelings spread through her; she turned away.

It took a moment for Bea to get her own emotions under control, and to remind herself that she had a life and a real job back in London. Despite the fact that

Amy had been reassuring in an email—they had an excellent team of staff who would be able to continue to work to the high standards required by the London Connection's clients while Amy, Clare and Bea were away—she still knew she needed to get back at the end of the month. There was no guarantee Matthaios would be out of rehab by then, despite what Ares hoped. If Bea could leave Danica with someone like Ellen then she'd have the peace of mind of knowing Danica was being not just looked after—but loved.

'How often can you work?'

'Every day.' Ellen smiled sweetly, rocking Danica on her hip. 'I'm between jobs at the moment, so the timing is perfect.'

'Yes.' Bea's voice caught in her throat. She coughed to cover it. 'I really need help through the day, so that I can get some work done.'

'You're a lawyer?' Ellen said curiously.

Bea nodded. 'Not the kind that goes to court though. I think it sounds more exciting than it is.'

Danica made a little noise then, and one chubby arm extended, reaching for Bea. Her heart turned over in her chest, the sense of being wanted and needed by Danica making her ache.

For a moment, Bea resisted. The longing to feel wanted was always followed by the knowledge that she wasn't—and that would happen here too. While Danica seemed dependent on Bea now, she knew that when she left Porto Heli the baby would have Ellen and Ares, and then Matthaios. Her life would continue without Bea, whereas she would always think of—and miss—the little baby who had so quickly worked her way into Bea's heart.

She wanted to resist out of a need for self-preservation, but those damned maternal instincts had her crossing the room and taking the baby from Ellen's arms. Danica put her little head on Bea's shoulder.

'Why don't I give you a tour of the house?'

An hour later, all the terms had been agreed. Ellen was going to spend several hours a day with Danica, and more if needed. She was helpful, flexible and had a kind nature. Bea told herself she was glad, even when she knew that with the admission of Ellen into the household staff, Ares's need for Bea lessened dramatically. It was a very good thing, then, that she was keeping a level head and not allowing their insane sexual chemistry to make her want more than was on offer.

CHAPTER ELEVEN

'It's so beautiful here.' Bea sighed appreciatively at the colours lighting up the sky—pink, purple, grey and silver, as the sun dipped closer to the horizon, preparing to draw a blanket of stars overhead. But for now it was a stunning display of dusk, her favourite time of the day, and Bea's soul drank it in.

They'd watched a week's worth of sunsets together since the first night they'd shared. By unspoken agreement, a rhythm had formed to their lives. Ares worked long days, often in his Athens office, returning after Danica was in bed. Bea worked when she could; despite Ellen's presence, she tried to limit herself mostly to Danica's nap time, so that she could be involved in the baby's life, and be sure things were running smoothly.

There was no cause for concern with Ellen. The young woman was calm and enthusiastic at the same time, an excellent companion for an energetic baby.

Bea's phone buzzing caught her attention. She reached behind her, swishing the screen to life, her pulse firing up when she saw a message from Amy.

'Bad news?' Ares's voice was deep and husky.

Bea read the message, her frown deepening.

Sorry I've been MIA. Try not to stress about what you're seeing in the papers—I'm okay. It's nothing like last time. I'll explain everything face to face. Love you. X

She didn't have the heart to tell her friend—a PR exec—that she hadn't read a newspaper headline since she'd been in Greece.

'Not bad news, I don't think…' She shook her head, quickly googling her friend's name and gasping when she read the first headline that appeared.

Palace Scandal! History repeats itself with new Lothario-in-Chief!

'Oh, no, Amy!'

She skimmed the text, baffled by the revelation of Amy's relationship with the Prince of Vallia. Last Bea had heard, Amy was going there in a professional capacity. So what was going on? This wasn't exactly good PR for the prince. She clicked into another article, shaking her head, reminding herself that Amy's text had explicitly said she was okay. It went some of the way to assuaging Bea's worries. Besides, there was no way Amy would get involved with a guy like Luca Albizzi. Not after last time.

Nonetheless, she hit the forward button on her phone and sent the article to Clare. Speaking of MIA, she'd heard nothing from the third member of their trio, but

Clare had said she'd likely be unavailable for a while, so that was hardly surprising.

Trying to ignore the *frisson* of worry, Bea brought herself back to the present, focusing on the warmth of the sun on her arms, the colours in the sky and, of course, the man in the pool.

Ares drew closer to the coping, his dark hair a wet pelt against his head. She watched the way the droplets rippled over his shoulders, admiring his tanned flesh and muscled arms.

'You're sure you won't join me?'

Her smile was wry. 'As I've told you every time you've asked, it's way too cold for swimming.'

He laughed. 'It's warm, I promise.'

On previous nights the evening had brought a chill breeze, but tonight there was more heat in the air. Though summer was still another six weeks away, the promise of its warmth surrounded them tonight.

'I'll compromise by sitting at the edge. Deal?'

He didn't say anything, simply watching her in that intense way of his as she stood, strolling towards him then sitting down. The denim miniskirt left her bare legs free to dangle in the water, the oversized tee required a pushing-up of the sleeves.

'How was work?' She reached out, ruffling his hair with her fingers, a jolt of anticipation running through her at the ease with which she could touch him, a man who had so recently appeared into her life and made her feel inadequate and powerful all at once.

His frown was infinitesimal. 'Busy,' he said, his eyes probing hers for a minute before he looked away.

Her heart skipped a beat as, for the first time in a week, she felt something akin to insecurity whisper through her. It was as though he was hiding something from her. As always, Bea was on the alert, looking for signs that a person she cared about was losing interest in her, ready to jump before she was pushed. How often she'd employed those skills with her parents—reading them intently, leaving a room before they could suggest she go and find something else to do, pretending occupation with a book so she wouldn't appear to notice the way they fawned over the twins, hanging on their every word.

'Ellen is doing well with Danica,' she said, to lay the groundwork for that possibility. If he wanted her to go, she wouldn't put up a fight. She'd make it easy for him, and walk away with her head held high. Worse than being unwanted, she'd learned a long time ago, was losing one's pride along with it.

'Yes.' The agreement was distracted, as though something important was on his mind.

Danger signs blared and, despite her intention to stay cool, panic gripped her heart.

'In all honesty, she could probably move in, you know.' *Say it, coward*, she urged herself. Clearing her throat, she forced an over-bright smile to her face. 'You could even release me from my kidnapping early.' She let the words hover between them, the suggestion that she would be completely fine with that.

'What?' His drawn-together brows showed confusion, as though it was the last thing he was expecting her to say.

'We agreed to a month before Ellen entered into the equation, and when Danica seemed much less settled,' Bea pointed out quietly. 'She's like a different baby now. You don't really need my help any more.'

The words were a form of acid in her throat. She tried to hold his eyes, to look brave and unconcerned, but she couldn't. She focused on the water instead, blinking several times to push back an overwhelming rush of emotion.

'We agreed to a month.' The words cracked around them harshly. 'I expect people I do business with to uphold their end of a deal. Are you trying to renege on our agreement?'

It was the reassurance she craved but in the strangest possible sense. This was so much more than business... wasn't it?

Doubts and uncertainties warred within her. She had no experience with men to compare this to, no idea what she'd wanted him to say. It was an indication that he didn't want her to leave though. Shouldn't that be enough?

'I'm not reneging,' she denied and, despite her best efforts, the words were softened by hurt.

He swore in his native tongue, coming to stand between her knees, looking up at her face intently. 'Do you want to go home?' he prompted, his own expression impossible to interpret. He was evidently far better at shielding his emotions than she was hers.

Home.

It was a strange word to employ, because it spoke of a sense she'd never known in her heart. Only as Ares asked the question did Bea realise she'd never actually thought of anywhere as home.

'I will not keep you here against your will.' The words seemed cut from glass, each sharp and cold, with the power to wound. But to wound who? His voice softened. 'And I will not sever my relationship with the London Connection. You do not need to stay because you're afraid of repercussions.'

It wasn't losing his business she was afraid of now; it was losing herself.

'Did you ever intend to fire the agency?' she asked quietly, moving her gaze to his face.

'Clare has managed my interests better than I can imagine anyone else doing,' he admitted finally. 'I never let my personal feelings enter into a business decision. Having made a single mistake in two years would have been a pretty poor reason to fire her.'

Bea's heart felt strangely light. 'So you were just using Clare's absence as leverage over me?'

He lifted his fingertips from the pool, dribbling a little water over her knee. 'I use whatever tools are at my disposal to achieve what I want.'

'And what did you want?'

'To get to know you better.'

Her ears were filled with a rush of noise like a tidal wave. 'Why?'

His frown was swift; she almost missed it. 'I can't say.'

'Why not?'

'I mean I don't know,' he corrected quietly. 'You were different, somehow.'

'Different to what?'

He braced his hands on the pool coping, pushing up effortlessly and holding himself there, a feat of abdominal control that even in that moment she didn't fail to notice. 'I was fascinated by you,' he corrected, brushing her lips with his, sending arrows of need through her body, arrows that almost drove all other thoughts from her mind. 'You were a contradiction and I wanted to understand that.'

He dropped back into the pool, resting his arms over her legs.

'And do you now?'

'No,' he answered immediately. 'If anything, the more I get to know you, the less sense you make.'

Her hazel eyes flared wide, surprised by that analysis. 'I think you're looking too hard. I'm actually very simple.'

His laugh was disbelieving. 'Liar.'

She dipped her fingertips into the pool, dribbling water over his shoulder before dropping her hand to his flesh, tracing invisible circles there.

'Stay the full month,' he said quietly, his eyes probing hers. 'So that I have more opportunity to make sense of you.'

It wasn't exactly what she needed to hear—no one had ever managed to offer Bea that—but it was enough. Enough for now to stave off her basic insecurities, to make her feel that he really did want her with him. He wasn't looking for an excuse to push her away; he wasn't counting down the minutes until she could leave. And even though he had Ellen to help with Danica, he still wanted Bea to be a part of their lives. For now.

* * *

'What is that song you sing to her?' Ares asked later that same night, when Bea was almost asleep. Her eyes were heavy and it took her mind a moment to wade back from the drugging proximity of sleep. Her body felt as though it was glowing, pleasure spreading through her limbs as the way he'd made her feel earlier set her pulse racing.

She hadn't been back to the guest room since the first night they'd made love. They hadn't discussed it; this had simply evolved out of a mutual need to be together at night, a desire to hold and touch, to wake up and reach for one another, satiating themselves over and over...

'Which song?' she asked sleepily. She flicked a glance to the bedside table. It had just passed midnight. Not terribly late but, given the way they were spending their nights, she was snatching sleep wherever she could find it.

His own voice was low and deep, so that when he hummed the familiar tune to Bea it sounded somehow mystical and different. She caught her breath, unused to hearing the song from anyone else.

'It's called "Calon Lân",' she murmured, turning in the bed so she could face him, resting her head on the pillow. 'It's Welsh.'

'You speak Welsh?'

'No.' Sadness etched her smile. She'd never told another soul why she knew that song, and yet the words bubbled through her now, pulling her towards him. 'I used to hum it as a girl—just a few lines, all that I could remember. For a long time, I didn't consciously know where it had come from, nor why I sang it. My adoptive dad, Ronnie, recognised the tune and played the full song for me.'

'Where did you learn it?'

Her heart skipped a beat. A pain that was almost too raw to speak of sliced through her. But Bea was nothing if not brave; confronting pain head-on was something she'd had to do enough times to be able to face it now.

'It's the only memory I have of my birth mother,' she said quietly. 'It's not even a memory,' she corrected, 'so much as a fog. A haze. If I think on it too hard it's like trying to catch soap in the bath—slippery and impossible. I can't remember what she looked like, and I can't remember anything about my life before…before I came to live with Ronnie and Alice—' her voice was rushed '—but I know she used to sing the song to me. She must have done it often, because it's kind of imprinted inside of me. And when I sing it I can feel her arms around me. I know that sounds strange.'

He shook his head once, just enough to disabuse her of that idea. 'Memory is a funny thing.'

'Yes.' She bit down on her lip. 'When I heard Danica crying, the words just came out of me. It's always comforted me, the song, and I thought it might do the same for her.'

'It appears to work wonders.'

She nodded, pressing her palm to his chest, feeling the steady rhythm of his heartbeat.

'What happened to your birth parents?'

She realised she'd been afraid of this question. No one had ever asked it. Amy and Clare had always instinctively understood that it was a no-go area. It was an almost impossible thing to reveal, because it was like admitting to someone that you just weren't very lovable.

'They didn't want me.' The words burned their way through her heart. She clamped her lips together in an attempt to stem any more.

A crease formed between his brows as he analysed that statement. 'For what reason?'

And there he'd found the crux of the matter. She laughed uneasily, flipping onto her back and staring at the ceiling. 'I was a difficult child, I guess.'

She couldn't look at him, so didn't see his reaction.

'It's fine,' she lied. 'They did the right thing and gave me away, obviously expecting I'd end up with a family more capable of caring for me.'

The silence that fell was barbed. 'And did you?'

Another question she'd never been asked, but this time because Amy and Clare had been able to see the truth for themselves. 'I grew up with everything you could want.' Her voice had a practised tone to it—the same one she'd used whenever people had enthused about how 'lucky' she was to have rock royalty for a dad and a bona fide supermodel as a mum.

'Why do I suspect that's not true?'

Damn him! She didn't want to talk about this. 'Are you kidding? Who wouldn't want to be raised by a couple of celebrities?'

'Lots of people,' he answered simply. 'And definitely you.'

Her throat thickened with emotion.

'You hate attention,' he said gently. 'And yet, given

their fame, I imagine you received more than your fair share.'

His perceptiveness knocked her off-balance, so she turned her face to his, her eyes wide.

'It was a strange way to grow up,' she agreed, careful not to reveal more than was necessary. 'They thought they couldn't have kids, so I was spoiled rotten when I first came to live with them.'

Most people would focus on that, wanting the details of just how much people like Ronnie and Alice would give their daughter. People were, in Bea's opinion, always obsessed with the minutiae of a celebrity's life—how were they like 'normal' people and in what ways did they differ?

Not Ares. He wasn't so easily diverted by the mention of fame and fortune.

'And then she fell pregnant and everything changed for you,' he prompted, recalling their earlier conversation, on the night they'd arrived at Porto Heli.

'In many ways.' She lifted one shoulder. 'Anyway, as I said, I really don't like to talk about my family.'

'I let you get away with that once, but not again.'

She blinked, surprised.

'I want to understand you,' he reminded her. 'And I suspect this is at the root of your mystery.'

'There is no mystery,' she demurred with a quick shake of her head.

'Why did you decide to study law?'

The subject change was so swift it almost gave her whiplash.

'I was good at it.'

It was a throwaway comment but the expression on his face showed something else, as though he was sliding another piece of a puzzle into place. She angled her face, hating the sensation of being a bug beneath his microscope.

'I imagine you received a lot of praise for that,' he said thoughtfully.

Bea pulled her lips to the side. 'I don't know what that's supposed to mean.'

'You received accolades for your academic achievements?'

'I mean, I graduated with a first, so in that sense, yes.'

'And your parents? They were proud?'

The pain was as fresh as when she'd called to tell them her results and her mother had spoken over the top of her to announce that Amarie had started dating a Hollywood actor.

'We think they might get engaged soon! He's so delicious, darling.'

'Of course they were,' she lied.

Without even turning to look at him, she knew he didn't believe her.

'Are you someone for whom good grades came easily?' he asked.

'No.' Oh, how she hated the bitter tears that were flooding her throat. She swallowed desperately. 'I suppose I have a bent for the law—it came more easily to me than, say, mathematics did. My mind definitely works a certain way. But I studied hard, to the exclusion of everything else. I was determined to—'

He waited for her to finish the sentence.

'To do well,' she finished lamely, not wanting to admit to him that making her parents proud had indeed formed a huge part of her motivation.

'And you did,' he said gently. It wasn't praise. It wasn't congratulations. And yet hearing him say those words warmed some small part of her, so she blinked her eyes and smiled, a weak smile pulled from her soul.

'Thank you.'

He lifted a hand, running it over her hair, his eyes following the movement of his fingers. 'I used to look at people like you and think you had it all. I would jealously watch university students with their books and rucksacks, their easy lives, and wish more than anything that I could trade places. I desperately wanted to be able to study. I thought people like you had it so easy.'

'Compared to you, I did,' she murmured softly.

'I don't know if that's true.' He moved closer, his lips brushing hers. 'There are many things besides food that people starve for, *agápi mou*.'

CHAPTER TWELVE

BEA WAS BEYOND worried about Amy. The last time they'd spoken, everything had been fine. Sure, the conversation was rushed, but Bea had presumed Amy was just caught up with work. But now Amy was back in London and her first order of business had apparently been to send this email. Bea read it again, shaking her head at Amy's request: Fire me, before this scandal gets out of hand. It made no sense, and all Bea could think was that she needed to speak to Amy, to tell her she loved her and would always support her. There was no way anyone was getting fired, no matter what had happened!

'Where are you? When are you coming back?' Amy asked when Bea called to reiterate her support. But before Bea could brush the question aside and bring the focus back onto Amy's email, Amy had a text from her demanding mother and had to abruptly end the call.

Bea's placed her phone down with a growing sense of disquiet.

The following week was the first time Ares had been allowed to see his brother and the visit brought with it a maelstrom of emotion. Matthaios looked good, but still, it was impossible for Ares to shake his sense of anxiety, as though he might say or do the wrong thing and set Matthaios back in his recovery. He felt as though he must walk a mile on eggshells.

'Who's the woman in the photo?' Matthaios asked conversationally, pointing to the image of Bea on Ares's phone.

Ares's eyes were drawn to her face, the affection she felt for Danica obvious in every line of her body. From the way she cradled Danica so completely, to the look in her eyes as she stared at the baby's dimpled face.

'Just someone who's helping me care for her,' Ares hedged uncomfortably. After all, that was the primary purpose of having Bea at Porto Heli. Never mind that they'd also spent the past three weeks exploring each other's bodies and minds to the point where she was almost all he could think of.

Not that Ares would ever really let a woman have that kind of control over him. He was focused on his work, on Matthaios, and now on Danica. That was it.

'*Theós*, she looks like her mother.'

For a moment Ares thought Matt meant Bea, who bore no resemblance to Ingrid whatsoever, except, he conceded, for their slender frames. But Ingrid had been so Danish, with her white-blonde hair and sky-blue eyes. Belatedly, he understood. Matt only had eyes for Danica. He was staring at the phone so hard it was possible a hole might burst through it.

'I will ask your doctors if I'm allowed to bring her

here,' Ares said firmly. 'You're doing so well, Matt. You seem like yourself again.'

Matthaios looked to his older brother, shaking his head slowly. 'Don't bring her to this place. It's bad enough that I'm here,' he muttered, dragging a hand through his hair. 'I don't mean that I don't need to be here. I know that I do. But I don't want Danica to see me like this.'

'She's barely six months old,' Ares reminded Matthaios. 'I don't think she'll mind that it's somewhat lacking in charm.'

'I'll mind,' he said.

'I think she misses you.'

'She deserves so much better.'

Ares's sigh was heavy, drawn from deep inside. He'd been reflecting on that lately—the bond between children and their parents or carers, the people put on this earth to keep them safe. For them, that had been their grandfather, and when he'd died they'd been cast out on their own, needing to fend for themselves. Their grandfather had died but the lessons he'd taught them remained. Ares knew that was where his resilience and determination had come from: mornings spent battling harsh weather and frigid temperatures, pulling ropes out of the ocean until calluses had formed across his palm, never once complaining or even remarking on the difficulties of that life.

'I think she's doing okay,' Ares commented.

'Thanks to you. Ares to the rescue, as always.'

But Matt was wrong. Ares wasn't coming to the rescue. He was simply cleaning up his own mess—fixing something that would never have been a problem in the first place if he'd done a better job of looking after Matt and Danica.

'Is she from an agency?'

Ares didn't immediately follow.

'I thought you said Cassandra was the last nanny they'd send you, after all the nannies I fired or shouted at.'

'No.' He shook his head. 'She's…a friend.'

'Oh.' Matthaios regarded the screen with more attention and now Ares wanted to flick the image away. A possessive heat ran through him. Not possessive of Beatrice so much as of what was happening between them. He wasn't prepared to discuss it; that felt like a betrayal. What they were sharing was inside a bubble, separate from time, and from their normal lives. Though they'd never agreed to keep it a secret, it just felt right.

'We've worked together. She saw how much I was struggling and offered to help out.'

'I see.'

Damn it, Ares suspected Matthaios *did* see. Having grown up so near in age and enduring most of life's adventures at each other's side, their relationship was very close, and Matthaios understood Ares better than anyone.

'Will I get to meet this friend of yours?'

'No.' The answer was swift and definitive. 'She must return to London next week. A month was all she could give Danica, I'm afraid.'

He ignored the swift stabbing sensation beneath his ribs.

'I don't know when I'll be out, Ares. Are you sure she can't stay longer?'

'Take all the time you need. Beatrice has hired a local girl who is also very good with the baby. Ellen dotes on her and will be available to help even when you return home. Someone who can ease you back into normal life.'

'And keep an eye on me, you mean?' Matt demanded sharply, briefly taking Ares back to the god-awful time shortly after Ingrid's death, when every question had led to an angry retort from his younger brother.

Matthaios winced apologetically. 'I know you mean well. I just hate…being here and having no…'

'Control,' Ares supplied, before his brother could even finish his sentence. 'I understand how you feel.' He could think of nothing worse than losing control of any situation, ever. 'What you have to realise is that in getting well you are taking control back. Control over the addiction that will chew through your life if you let it, just as it did our mother's.'

'I know that.' Matt's eyes fired with courage. 'I'm not going to mess this up, Ares.' He looked to the phone once more. 'She means too much to me.'

'You're very quiet.'

He regarded Bea over the rim of his glass. She was wearing the dress he'd chosen from the department store. He'd grabbed it simply because it had been nearby but, seeing it on her now, the colours were the perfect palette to draw out her complexion.

'Am I?' The question was designed to stall. She was right; he had been preoccupied since returning from visiting Matthaios.

'You've answered in monosyllables practically all evening.' Concern clouded her eyes. 'Is everything okay?'

He fingered the stem of his wine glass. 'I saw Matt today. My brother.' And then, as though she couldn't connect the dots. 'Danica's father.'

Her smile showed how redundant his second two statements had been. 'How is he?'

'Doing better,' Ares admitted. 'Frustrated that it's taking longer than expected to feel back to full health.'

'What do the doctors say?'

'That he should take as long as he needs, but that he's showing very promising signs for a meaningful recovery. It's never a smooth journey, though. It will require lifelong vigilance, so now it's about arming him with the tools to recognise when he's at risk of relapsing, as well as how to surround himself with people who are good for him.'

'What was Danica's mother like?'

Ares's smile came easily. 'An excellent influence. He adored her, and she didn't let him get away with anything. I abhor the idea of soulmates,' he said with an unintended shudder, 'but in this case I would willingly make an exception.'

'Are you so sceptical about love?' she asked, and although he knew she was determined to get back to her life in London he felt a natural throb of concern enter his bloodstream. This was the longest he'd ever spent with a woman. Ares always, without fail, left before things could get beyond the first flush of sexual chemistry. He had no interest in growing dependent on anyone, and even less in being needed.

If this time had proved anything, though, it was that he was stronger than he'd thought. Three weeks with Bea had flown by and while they'd been thoroughly enjoyable, he had no difficulty in accepting their affair was almost at an end. Oh, he'd miss her, but just in a physical way, and that wouldn't last long, surely.

'Love is fine,' he said with a careful smile. 'For Matthaios it was necessary. Ingrid changed him and even though her death destroyed a part of him, he is still a better man for having loved her.'

'But it's not for you,' she pushed, her own expression giving frustratingly little away.

'Love requires commitment and I have always preferred to be alone.'

'Why?'

'This, coming from you?'

Her grimace might have been an attempt at a smile.

'My career is my life,' she said.

He understood her drive and determination. He had always been motivated by a similar need to achieve.

'As a child, I knew that Matthaios's life was inextricably linked to mine. His success was mine to encourage. His failures landed at my feet. When my grandfather died, he left just the two of us, and Matt became dependent in a way that has haunted me ever since. I've let him down too many times, Beatrice.'

'I'm sure he wouldn't share your assessment.'

'Be that as it may, it's how I feel. I would never want anyone else to depend on me. Not a woman, not a child. No one.'

She reached for her own drink, sipping it slowly, her eyes showing she was lost in thought.

He couldn't say why, but he wanted her to understand. 'Dependence is…difficult,' he said with a shake of his head. 'My mother…' Was he really going to go down this path?

'Yes?'

His eyes locked on hers on a sigh of frustration. 'I couldn't help her. I loved her—I was just a kid and she was my mother—but it didn't matter what I said or did.'

Beatrice was frowning. 'What was she like?'

'Fun.' His grimace showed pain. 'When she was around, at least. She was full of energy some of the time, taking us to the playground at midnight or sneaking us in to see a movie, spontaneous and—' He sought the word.

'Erratic?' she supplied gently.

'Yes. Exactly. I realise now that this "spontaneous" fun usually coincided with her benders. Then the darkness would come—days of her being in bed, unable or unwilling to move. Sick, shouting at us to be quiet.'

'And so you took care of her?'

'As much as she'd let me.' He shrugged.

'And Matthaios?'

'Yes. I cared for him too. Someone had to feed him.'

Bea's eyes were filled with sympathy. He looked away, firming his jaw.

'So you can see why I'm sceptical about the whole idea of being needed by anyone. It's not healthy. I hate it.'

Bea's soft exhalation of breath eventually drew his gaze back.

'Anyone else might say that sounds kind of lonely,' she observed eventually.

Something strengthened in his chest. 'But not you?'

She shook her head slowly. 'No. Not me.'

For himself, he understood the decision, but for Bea, something inside Ares cracked apart a little. There was something completely unacceptable about the way she'd walled herself off from life and the experience of companionship.

He reached across the table, putting his hand on hers. 'I don't get seriously involved with the women I date, Beatrice, because I abhor the idea of relationships and all the emotional expectations that come from them. But I *do* date. I enjoy the company of women, I enjoy sex and intimacy. I appreciate the importance of human connection, even when I know I have my limits.'

Her smile was wry. 'I don't think that's any better than the way I live my life.'

'So when you leave here, is it your intention to go back to the way things were before? Avoiding men, avoiding dating, hiding yourself in unflattering outfits lest someone actually recognises that you're a sensual, attractive woman?'

Her cheeks turned a vibrant pink, her lips parting indignantly. 'That's not—' She clamped her lips down on the denial. 'That's none of your business.'

He laced their fingers together, squeezing her hand. 'You deserve better than the life you're living.'

She pulled her hand away. 'I like my life.'

He didn't need to say anything to challenge her. His look communicated his scepticism just fine. She huffed and stood, pacing towards the pool. As the evenings had grown warmer they'd taken to eating out here. Beatrice, Ares had learned, loved sunsets, her affinity with this time of day something he'd subconsciously begun to crave. He'd made sure he was home in time to enjoy them with her—or, rather, to enjoy her enchantment as the sky dressed itself in a different outfit each evening. Tonight had been cloudless, so the sky had filled with a gentle gradient, fading from purple at the horizon to gold and peach. The ocean took on tones to match, a steely turquoise in the lessening light.

He pushed his own chair back. Nothing he'd said had been wrong, but upsetting Bea was intolerable. He prowled towards her, standing at her back, his hands curving over her shoulders.

'It's your life,' he murmured gently. 'And in less than a week you'll get back to it. I don't like to think of you leading it alone—even when, selfishly, a part of me never wants you to get involved with any other man.'

He felt her sharp intake of breath and laughed. 'Don't worry. I'm not suggesting that we continue this. It's pure male ego.'

She exhaled slowly. 'What if…'

The words were so soft he barely caught them. 'Yes?'

She turned in the circle of his arms, her eyes looking deep into his own, stirring something in his soul. 'What if, after this week's over, we still…see each other?' The muscles of her throat bunched delicately. 'From time to time,' she added quickly.

It was like being split apart by the stroke on an anvil. There was danger here. Danger in the way Beatrice provoked him, spoke to him, pushed him—danger in the sweet little noises she made when they slept together, danger in the fact that he'd already spent more time with her than he had with any other woman. If maintaining control was the most important thing in his life, then Bea represented a very real threat to that.

He ground his teeth together, mentally distancing himself. 'That's not possible.'

He saw the hurt in her eyes briefly before she let them drift shut, her lashes forming two dark velvet fans against her cheeks. 'Why not?'

'Because it would just be prolonging the inevitable. I won't let you waste your life like that.'

'It's my life,' she pointed out defiantly.

'And my conscience to live with.' He regarded her warily, hating that she was trying to move the parameters of their safe agreement.

She turned away from him abruptly so he had no idea of her reaction to those words.

He had to drive his point home. 'Bea, I like sex. I like it a lot. These last few weeks have been…better than I could have imagined. But we both knew it would end.'

Silence grew thick between them. When she spoke, her voice was stiff like iron, but quieter than the whispering wind, so he had to lean closer to catch the words.

'This isn't a protestation of love. I'm just saying we could—casually—see each other when I'm back in London. If you want to.'

Why did he hate that even more? Why did he want to shout that a no-strings relationship like that wasn't good enough for her?

It was a double standard; if she wanted to limit herself to that kind of relationship—just as he did—then that was her choice.

But Bea was different to him.

Where Ares had grown hard and ruthless out of habit and necessity, Bea was soft and sweet, vulnerable beneath a thin outer layer that imitated coldness. She wasn't cold though, and she wasn't someone who was suited to live her life alone. She was just too scared to let herself love anyone.

He clamped his jaw, turning her gently and catching her hands, lifting them to his chest. She didn't quite meet his eyes.

'I want to enjoy the time we have left, and then I want you to leave my home and never look back. Don't think about me, don't think about Danica. Go home and start your life over—only promise me that you'll keep an open mind about companionship. You deserve better than to keep pushing everyone away, *agápi mou*.'

Pain was slashing through her. A pain that was familiar and intense.

He didn't want her.

He didn't want her.

The words kept circling through her brain, prickly and sharp, so she had to bite back a groan. Her insides were awash with acid but Bea wouldn't let him see her pain. Just like she'd learned to hide it from her parents, and from everyone else, she hid it from Ares now, flicking him a careless smile even as something inside her was shattering into a thousand pieces.

He didn't want her.

'I'll grant you most of what you've asked for,' she said gently.

He was very still and that stillness was all the confirmation she needed. He'd never want her. No one would.

'I won't think about you when I leave...' the words caught in her throat a little '...but Danica will always have a place in here.' She pulled her hand free and pressed it to her heart. 'I can't promise I won't think of her often.'

It wasn't just sunset that Bea loved; it was sunrise too. The bookends of the day that broke across the sky, rendering it with a sense of magic and newness, the promise of a new dawn and new hope.

The next morning she pushed back the sheets of Ares's bed and crept out silently, steeling herself to recognise that this was almost over. Soon there would be no more waking up beside him, no more pressing back against his naked body, teasing him with her proximity, silently pleading with him to make love to her again. There was only a handful of nights left to enjoy Ares, and then she'd never see him again. Because he didn't want her.

The sand was cold beneath her feet, and damp from the receding waves' kiss. She walked slowly at first, her arms wrapped across her chest, her eyes on the distant stars in the sky, each dwindling by the second, losing their sparkle as light permeated their backdrop.

Her first thought should have been of Danica. The little girl who'd lost her mother, and in some ways her father too, who'd been sent to live with an uncle who'd outsourced her care because he didn't know how to accommodate her in his life and heart. The little girl who had calmed at the first sign of real love and understanding. Her first thought should have been of the baby, but it wasn't. Though she would miss Danica like an absent limb, her feelings for Ares were so much more complex.

She could admit how she felt about Danica. She could understand every single emotion she had for the baby. The sense of affection, of protectiveness, her amusement at the little faces Danica pulled—everything there made sense.

She felt, Bea supposed, as one was meant to when confronted with an adorable, helpless, dependent, sweet infant. She loved her.

It was simple and made sense, whereas everything she felt for Ares was a Dumpster fire of doubt. Physically, she understood what she wanted. He was gorgeous and he made her feel as though she were floating. She could never have counted how many orgasms they'd shared, but that wasn't the whole story. This was more than just sex. It was the way his leg brushed hers beneath the dinner table each evening, the way he held her vice-like, clamped to his chest as he slept, as though he needed to exhale and inhale with the same rhythm she did. It was the way he reached for her hand when they walked, or watched her as she did something as banal as making coffee. It was the way she'd felt that first morning when she'd seen him holding Danica and a wound in her heart had started to stitch back together.

But beyond the physical it was all so murky and uncertain.

She knew she didn't want to do as he'd suggested the night before. She didn't want to walk away from him and forget he existed. She didn't want to live without him in her life.

The realisation made her gasp. She stopped walking, shocked into an inability to put even one foot in front of the other. It shouldn't have surprised her so much; wasn't that what she'd been suggesting last night? Hadn't she tried to find a way to maintain some form of relationship with Ares?

And he'd shut her down. Pushed her away. Oh, he'd done it so well, so beautifully, so *kindly*, as though he really cared about hurting her feelings, but the root cause had been the same. He wanted her to leave at the agreed upon time. He wanted her to leave and never contact him again.

He wanted her out of his life.

Her fist lifted and pressed against her mouth, blocking the sob that was welling in her chest.

Everything Bea had ever read about adoption had spoken of the total unwavering love and commitment an adoptive parent felt for their adopted child—the fact that most wouldn't make the distinction between biological and adopted. That hadn't been the case for her. Not only had her adoptive parents acted as though they regretted bringing her into their lives, her mother had frequently said as much. Not in so many words—Alice was too delicate for that—but she'd made it abundantly clear how she felt.

Like the time a photographer from a glossy magazine had come to the house to take photos to accompany an article they were featuring, and Alice had sent Bea to the study, suggesting it would be better with 'just the real family'. She'd been thirteen years old, home from school for a brief holiday, and the phrase hadn't made sense at first, then it had filtered into her brain like a thunderstorm at its peak, screeching and whirling with the force of a tornado. She'd gone to her room and cried, but out of those tears a determination had formed. She'd sworn she'd never let Alice hurt her again.

Oh, that hadn't been possible. Though Bea tried to be hard-hearted, she wasn't. Naturally she was soft and loving, and every insult and exclusion from the only people she thought of as family lashed her like a whip at her spine.

It wasn't only their cruelty that had cut her, though. It was their volatility. When Alice had wanted the world to see her as a compassionate, altruistic doyenne of charitable acts, she'd brought out Bea for everyone to see, disregarding Bea's natural dislike for cameras and attention. At those times Alice appeared to dote on Bea, and Bea, so starved for affection and warmth, had lapped it up, craving more, wondering what she'd done to deserve the sudden spurt of affection. It would dissipate just as abruptly as it had emerged, Bea packed off back to boarding school, and weeks would pass without a call or text message from her parents.

Her spirit broke so many times over the years, she thought it had been destroyed beyond repair.

She thought she'd got to the point where she would

never again run the risk of being hurt. She'd pulled right back from her adoptive parents, deciding that she could play her part at Christmastime, visiting them for lunch and then speaking to Ronnie and Alice as equals—the less she expected of them, the better things went.

She'd grown out of wanting their love, and she'd told herself she'd never want *anyone's* love again. It was too dangerous, too likely to lead to emotional carnage, and God knew she'd suffered enough of that in her lifetime.

She sank down onto the sand; it was cold beneath her bottom. Staring out to sea, a wall of fear surrounded her, as vast as the ocean beyond this bay.

Despite everything they'd done to her, Bea loved her parents. She'd tried not to, but love wasn't something you could choose to feel or avoid. Love was as non-optional as breathing. And somewhere since meeting him, probably the night he'd stormed into the office, so cranky and unlike anyone she'd ever known before, Bea had fallen head over heels in love with Ares.

It was a disaster.

She knew without a shadow of a doubt that he would never love her back. And she knew intimately the pain that came from loving and not having that love returned.

If he felt anything for her whatsoever, he would have accepted her suggestion that they find a way to continue seeing one another, even after she went back to London. He hadn't. He didn't love her and that meant one thing and one thing only.

Bea had to escape.

CHAPTER THIRTEEN

HIS ARMS AROUND her waist were almost too perfect to bear. She allowed herself the weakness of sinking back into him just for a moment, one last sublime second of physical closeness, one last moment in which she could pretend that everything was just as it should be, before shattering the illusion with the truth.

Her heart stuttered in her chest, the enormity of what she was about to do dragging on her like a stone.

You could stay, a little voice in her head taunted. Stay for the rest of the week, enjoy the intimacy he was willing to offer, gather the crumbs of his affection for Afterwards, when he was no longer a part of her life and she needed to line her heart space with as many gold dust recollections as she possibly could.

At what cost?

Another sob welled in her chest and she pulled away from him, moving towards the corner of the kitchen, her palms pressed to the counter, her spine straight as she rallied every iota of strength she possessed. Fortunately, Bea had a lot of experience with difficult goodbyes, and even more with heartbreak.

'Beatrice?'

God, she loved how he used her full name. He was the only person who did, and the way he said it, with his accent, spiced with desire…

She swallowed, turning around and forcing her eyes to meet and hold his. She saw the speculation in them, and then the concern.

'Something's wrong.'

She'd asked Ellen to take Danica for a walk in the pram, having given the little baby a tight squeeze and a kiss on the tip of her nose, her heart breaking with the abundance of affection she felt for a child she had known for less than a month. So much for never wanting children! Never wanting to fall in love! What a fool she'd been to think she could dictate such basic human emotions.

'What is it?' He crossed the room, catching her hands in his, lifting them between them as he'd done the night before. It was a strange and fitting gesture, bridging their hearts in some way.

A thousand words swirled through her brain but she struggled to pluck the right assortment to form a sentence that would explain the realisation she'd had, and why that meant she had to leave immediately.

'When I graduated from university my parents sent their personal assistant to take photographs and give me a gift,' she said softly, recalling the delicate diamond bracelet in the turquoise box. 'The assistant was as awkward about it as I was devastated. He took the photos, gave me the gift and left as quickly as he could.' Her throat felt as though it were closing in on itself. 'I was so angry, Ares. It was a simple graduation ceremony only an hour's drive from their house, and they couldn't even make it. They didn't want to.'

He frowned, nodding slowly, though the reason for Bea divulging this obviously made little sense to him.

'My life has been filled with this horrible feeling of loving people who'll never love me back. Of knowing that nothing I do will ever make them proud, or even really make them aware that I exist. They supported me financially—they gave me anything I wanted materially—but they had, and still have, no idea who I really am. And yet I love them, because they're the closest thing to parents I've got.'

Her eyes swept shut as so many memories and hurts battered her, swelling within her, demanding to be shared.

'I know what it feels like to live in a void of uncertainty. Loving and not having that love returned is a horrible way to live, so I swore I'd never risk it. Why would anyone love me, anyway?'

His hands squeezed hers. 'Stop that. You know what an incredible woman you are. Any man would be lucky to have you.'

'Don't.' The word whipped between them, fierce and furious. 'Don't lie to me. Don't placate me with empty words.'

Surprise etched its way across his features.

'You say that but, as I've learned, words are cheap. It's easy to say one thing when you feel exactly the opposite.'

Something like proud defiance lit his eyes. 'I never say what I don't feel.'

'But you don't love me,' she challenged him.

His features grew taut, his lips tight.

'You say any man would be lucky to have me, but you don't want me. Are you not "any man"?'

'Beatrice…' He said her name like a plea, and her gut ached because this was all too familiar. How often she'd been made to feel guilty for complaining. Oh, not recently, but as a young girl, before she'd learned to accept the reality of her situation, when she'd still thought there could be an explanation for the inequities of her parents' treatment of her versus the twins, she'd argued for her cause, only to be made to feel as though she were being overly dramatic.

'Don't gaslight me,' she snapped, earning herself a look of complete shock.

He pulled his hands away, lifting his palms to her. 'I'm not. I'm simply trying to understand—'

He didn't finish the sentence. His brows drew together as he scanned her face, as though he might find answers there.

'What I suggested last night, about us seeing each other again after this week—it wasn't just because I enjoy having sex with you. I like being with you. I like spending time with you and getting to know you.' She shook her head with frustration. 'No, not getting to know you. I feel like on a soul-deep level I know everything there is to know about you. I feel like if it's possible that one person could be designed to fit perfectly with another person, then you're *my* person.'

His jaw shifted as though he were grinding his teeth together; he said nothing.

Bravely, she pushed on, her voice soft now, thick with emotion. 'I lied to you last night, Ares, but only because I've been lying to myself. It turns out I gave you my heart the first night we met, and I want you to keep it for ever.' She only became aware that a tear had slid down her cheek when it landed on her wrist.

'I can't believe this.' The words were short, his own emotions colouring the sentence so it emerged with obvious disappointment. 'I was so clear—'

'I know you were,' she agreed, a part of her withering at his clear-cut condemnation of how foolish she was being. 'But did you really think that would be enough?'

His eyes flared wide and something sparked in her chest. Hurting him felt good. What was wrong with her? How could she want to hurt the man she loved?

Because he was hurting her, and she was so tired of that. So tired of being hurt and ignored by the people she loved.

'Did you think that telling me I couldn't love you would mean a damned thing when you *invited* me, every single night we spent together, to do exactly that? Your words told me not to care but your body made it impossible not to.'

'That's just sex,' he said, but his voice was uneasy, guilt evident in every line of his face.

'Wow.' Now it was Bea's turn to feel pain—more pain than she'd known. 'Just sex. Good to know.'

'Beatrice, that isn't what I meant.'

'I thought you didn't say things you don't mean.'

He compressed his lips. 'Stop trying to trap me. I'm attempting to explain—'

'But that's just words again,' she interrupted, panic making her voice high-pitched. 'You say I can't love you, but do you even stop and think about whether or not you love me too?'

He wore a dismissive mask, his eyes glittering grey. 'I do not need to think about it.'

Her chest ached. Tears caused her throat to sting. 'So you don't love me.'

A muscle flexed near his jaw. 'I've said this from the first night.'

'Yes, yes,' she groaned. 'You did. But that was almost a month ago. Do you really still feel that way?'

He stared at her for several seconds and then nodded. 'Yes. It's exactly how I feel.'

He was being so clear and emphatic. Only a fool would continue this conversation when it could result in just one thing: more hurt. More rejection. Yet still she stood there, allowing the screws to be tightened, a glutton, apparently, for punishment.

'I came here wanting to hate you for kidnapping me, and then I saw you with Danica and I saw you with me and everything changed. I fell so completely in love with you, Ares.'

'Stop.' He shook his head. 'Stop saying that, Beatrice. It's a betrayal of everything we agreed. I don't want your love. I don't want you to need me. For God's sake, I don't want anything from you—got it?'

His outburst surprised them both. His words were so much more certain than she'd expected. She'd hoped for a hint of doubt. For a sign that on some level he might be torn, or starting to comprehend his true feelings. But this was adamant and determined. No one who felt even a hint of love could speak like that.

She angled her face away from him, the enormity of their situation and her error, first in loving him and second in telling him, spreading through her.

'Hurting you is the very last thing I wanted.'

She nodded slowly. 'Then why are you?'

'Do I have an alternative?'

She looked deep into his eyes, trying to fathom his meaning.

'I don't love you, Beatrice. Should I lie to you, just to avoid making you cry?'

Even now, his words were so cutting. Devastation wrapped around her. It wasn't only from what he was inflicting on her; it was the culmination of every feeling of worthlessness she'd ever known.

He cupped her cheek so gently that it was a lie in and of itself. His touch spoke of such tenderness and affection, yet he didn't feel those things for her.

'I don't love you, but not because you're unlovable, *agápi mou.*'

She dipped her eyes downwards, focusing on the floor between them, fresh pain scoring her heart. 'Then why not?'

She felt his gaze burning the top of her head and waited for an answer, an explanation, anything he could offer that would lessen the sting of this rejection.

'Because I'm not capable of it. And because it's not what I want.'

You're not what I want. So simple. So final.

She blinked rapidly, trying to clear her eyes of tears and her brain of the tangle of emotions. 'I have to get out of here.' It was a whispered resolution at first. Then stronger. 'I have to go home.' Home? What a farce.

'Yes.' His agreement was the final straw. She spun away from him just in time; her sob escaped with enough warning to muffle it completely. 'I'll have my jet fuelled up.'

'No.' It was an immediate visceral reaction. 'Not your jet.' She swallowed furiously. 'If you can just get me to Athens, I'll organise my own flight home.'

'Beatrice, be sensible. I have a plane on standby. It's no trouble.'

'No.' She shook her head to underscore how serious she was. Everything about his private jet would only remind her of him. She couldn't do it. 'I want to do this myself. Please.'

His eyes warred with hers. She felt he was about to argue and held her breath, reserving her energy for exactly that. But, to her surprise, he dipped his head in agreement. 'When would you like to leave?'

'I'm ready now.'

His eyes glittered, something like rejection in them, and a fierce dismissal of that, but again he nodded. 'I'll get Danica so that you can say goodbye.'

'I've already done that. Ellen's taken her for a walk.' Heat flushed her cheeks. 'I didn't want them to overhear our conversation.'

His eyes narrowed and she felt ice run the length of

her spine. 'You've thought of everything,' he remarked with stony reserve.

'Don't you dare make me the bad guy here.'

He stared at her, something tightening in his features before he sighed. 'I'm not. I'm well aware that title is completely mine.'

She could only stare at him, her heart in tatters at her feet, her soul withering deep inside her.

'Meet me on the roof when you're ready. I'll be waiting.'

It was an unconscious echo of the words he'd said on the day they'd gone shopping. So much had happened since then, he hadn't consciously evoked that time. But he'd thought of it again as he'd waited by the helicopter, watching her walk towards him holding only a garment bag which contained, he presumed, her ballgown. She brought no other bag, none of the clothes she'd accumulated whilst staying here.

He was both glad and sorry. Sorry because it showed how deeply he'd wounded her that Bea wasn't even able to take her own clothes, and glad because these physical items would serve as some kind of reminder of her. So that when he woke up at night and wondered if it had all been a dream, he'd see the clothes and know that, no, for a little while, he'd had Beatrice in his life.

And he could have her for longer, he argued with himself as she approached. All he had to do was ask her to be patient. To let him see if he could love her.

But he knew the answer already.

This wasn't about whether he could love Beatrice;

it was about whether he wanted her to love him. To depend on him. To rely on him for her happiness and safety. There had been someone relying on him since he was a young boy, and without fail he'd let them down. His mother, his brother, now Danica—he hadn't even been able to hire appropriate staff to care for her. The idea of Bea depending on him, only to realise what a terrible idea that was…to see her life turn to ashes as he failed her in some vital way?

No.

He couldn't bear that.

He'd let her go and, despite what she might think now, she'd get over him. She'd move on and because of the experience they'd shared she'd be more open to love with the right sort of man next time.

'Armandos will take you to the airport,' he said when she was almost level with him. 'Unless you would like me to come with you?'

She bristled visibly, moving her head to the side. 'I'd prefer to go alone.' Her smile was brittle. 'Thank you.'

Ever polite, he thought with a harsh twist in his gut.

'Beatrice?' He had no idea what he was going to say, but he knew it didn't feel right to let her leave like this.

'Thank you for everything. With Danica.'

Her eyes shifted to his shoulder. 'I loved spending time with her.' Her lower lip wobbled and he moved quickly, opening the door to the helicopter, understanding the small kindness he could show her now. She just wanted to escape. Trapping her here to talk was further proof of his inability to be the man she needed.

'Let me know when you're back in London,' he requested. 'So I know you arrived there safely.'

She grimaced. 'I'll be fine, Ares. You can start forgetting about me right now.'

What could he say to that? He'd practically boasted to her about that being the wise thing to do. He couldn't deny it now, or she might read something into it. But as the helicopter lifted off, becoming a distant, gleaming speck of black against an azure blue sky, he knew he'd never forget Bea, and strangely he was glad of that.

Bea was in a fog. She managed, somehow, to buy herself a ticket on the next plane leaving for London, and to contemplate sending Amy a quick text to let her know she'd be home soon. Except Bea didn't want to see Amy or Clare. For the first time in her adult life, Bea truly felt that she didn't want to talk to her best friends. Not about this. She simply needed to be alone.

Amy would know within seconds that something serious had happened, and Bea couldn't lie to one of her best friends. She had to be stronger before they had that conversation.

If Amy had been a less worthy friend it would have been possible to presume she'd be too wrapped up in her own life to notice anything amiss with Bea. But Amy was loyal, kind and compassionate and she'd likely take one look at Bea and realise that her heart had been shattered. Hell, she'd probably insist the London Connection drop Ares as a client after this, and Bea knew they couldn't afford that. She had to heal a bit before she saw either Amy or Clare again, knowing their loyal streaks would be invoked. No one was expecting her back in London for a few more days. She'd sneak home to her apartment and lie low, just until she was ready to drag her brave face back into place.

Decision made, she went through Security and waited near the boarding gate, trying not to think about Ares, about Danica, and about how much she was already missing them both.

It was a stunning sunset. All the colours streaked across the sky, the deepest oranges and reds with a shimmer of gold, purple glowing from behind the scant covering of silvery clouds. Ares stared at it and felt a gut-punch of sorrow. He was sorry that Bea wasn't with him; she'd have loved it. Sorry that they weren't going to see another sunset together.

Sorry that he'd hurt her so badly.

Sorry that he'd never see her again.

Just horribly, regrettably sorry.

She never texted or called to let him know she'd arrived in London but, given the lack of news about a plane crash or the kidnapping of a twenty-nine-year-old executive, he had to presume she'd made it there and chosen not to contact him. A wise decision, but he yearned to hear something from her. Just to know she was okay.

As a child, his grandfather had told him often that 'time heals all wounds', and Ares had generally felt there was truth in that. But the more time that separated him from Bea, the worse he felt. Danica was unsettled and, two days after Bea left, Ellen moved into a guest room so she could be available to help around the clock.

Ares took that as an opportunity to leave Porto Heli, where everything, everyone and everywhere, reminded him of Bea. He needed to get away from her, any way he could.

CHAPTER FOURTEEN

'Oh, my God.' She stared at the rapidly spreading stain of milky coffee against a broad chest, her heart in her throat as her eyes lifted higher to ascertain that, yes, somehow, surely in an alternative universe, Beatrice Jones had once again managed to spill her coffee all over Ares Lykaios's chest.

It made no sense. Her brain struggled to translate what she was seeing. She'd barely slept since returning from Athens four days earlier. She was living on a strange combination of Netflix and coffee from the coffee chain beneath her apartment. She didn't even have to order now; when the baristas saw her walk in they began to prepare her drink, so all she had to do was tap her credit card and grab it when it was ready.

And in the case of this, coffee number four for the day, slam it into the chest of the only man she'd ever loved.

'I swear I put on the lid.' But the fact that it had burst open the instant she'd bumped into him might make him beg to differ.

Oh, God. She looked terrible. She couldn't remember the last time she'd showered. Her hair was scraped back into a ponytail, her shirt had a stain on the sleeve and she'd abandoned make-up for the sheen of take-away noodle fumes.

'Beatrice.' He growled her name from somewhere deep in his throat and goosebumps ran across her skin; her stomach flipped. She looked at her watch for no logical reason except that time would tether her—she hoped—to reality. It was almost five in the afternoon. Of what day?

'What are you doing here?'

Of all the questions running through her brain, that was uppermost.

'I came to see you.'

Obviously. Why else would he be in this exact part of London? 'Is it Danica?' she asked quickly, concern for the little girl momentarily eclipsing anything else.

He flinched. 'Danica is fine. She's...at home with Ellen.' His lips were a grim smudge on his face.

'Oh. I'm glad.'

'May I come in?' He gestured to the security door to her building.

Bea stared at it, panic gripping her heart. She shook her head instinctively.

'Just for a moment.' There was something so imperative and commanding in his tone that Bea found herself sighing and moving towards it. She could control this situation. And she could definitely control how much she let him see of her pain. She had pride and she would use it to strengthen her resolve until he finally left. At the same time, she acknowledged that she desperately wanted him to stay. Seeing him under any circumstances was better than not, and oh, how hungry she was for the sight of him, the feel of him.

'How did you find out where I live?'

'It wasn't difficult.'

Of course it wasn't difficult for someone like Ares Lykaios. Somewhere during the time they'd spent together in Greece, she'd come to see him as a mere mortal, simply a man she'd fallen in love with, but he wasn't anything so pedestrian as that. He was powerful and could do whatever the hell he wanted.

She buzzed open the security door then gestured to the door at the top of the stairs, a shiny black with a golden number four emblazoned on it.

'There are two apartments downstairs,' she explained as she averted her gaze from him, knowing she couldn't watch as he walked up the stairs or desire would undo every effort she was making to hold onto her pride. 'But no apartment number three. I've always wondered if the original builders thought it was unlucky or something.' She clamped her lips together, aware she was filling the nervous silence with babble and hating herself for that.

At the door of her apartment she hesitated, her eyes darting to his before returning to the lock.

'Two minutes,' he commanded, and when she still didn't move he reached out and took the extended key from her fingertips and inserted it, pushing the door open with an expression that was inscrutable.

Bea's heart was in her throat, emotions running rampant. She wasn't prepared for this. She'd wondered if she'd ever see him again, but had presumed that she'd at least have time to brace for that, to prepare herself for the mental hurdle of being near him once more.

This was *hard*.

She fought ingrained good manners, pointing to a chair without offering him a drink. Despite the dark patch spreading over his shirt, she refused to do anything to accommodate him. She'd had enough of being trampled. Enough of putting her heart out there and having it unceremoniously refused.

Bea's apartment had a large open-plan kitchen and lounge area. She kicked off her shoes then padded into the all-white kitchen, depositing the almost empty coffee cup into the sink and washing her hands before slipping a pod into her own machine. The muscle memory of the task was reassuring and somewhat calming; his eyes on her as she did something so simple was not. The machine whirred as dark coffee began to run into the mug.

When she turned around, he was staring at her intently and her breath slammed through her. She wanted to stamp her foot and she realised her temper was running away from her. How dared he come here with no warning, looking so damned perfect? As though nothing in the world was bothering him. As though his life was continuing completely as normal.

'What are you doing here?' Pride be damned. The words were a husky groan, a plea for him to disappear again so she could continue getting over him.

His lips compressed. The coffee machine stopped whirring.

'I can't sleep.'

She stared at him, the words making no sense.

'Then you should go see a doctor. See if they'll prescribe you something.'

'It wouldn't help.'

'I'm sure it would.'

He shook his head. 'Every time I close my eyes I see your face on that last morning in Greece. I see the way you looked at me when you told me you loved me and I didn't say it back, and I feel as though something is being twisted in my chest, the blade of a dagger, I don't know. And then I'm wide awake again. I just…need to know that you're okay. That's all.'

Her heart stuttered. She turned away with the pretence of reaching for her coffee, cradling it in her hands, taking a perverse pleasure in denying him the same courtesy. It was childish, yet she didn't care.

'I'm fine.' Pride came to her rescue. She'd begged him to love her once. She wouldn't do it again.

He nodded slowly, his eyes scanning her face.

Please go. She couldn't handle this much longer.

'Fine.' He dragged a hand through his hair. 'Good.' He frowned. 'I'm…glad.'

He turned towards the door and took two steps in that direction then made a deep noise of frustration, pivoting to face her. His eyes pinned her to the spot, his features a mask of something she couldn't fathom. He stared at her long and hard, so the air between them became thick with unspoken words, and then he swore, a dark, throaty curse in his native Greek, a word that reverberated around her kitchen again and again.

'Damn it, Beatrice. I can't do this.'

She wasn't capable of speaking.

'I can't be the man you want me to be. Do you have any idea how much I want to give you what you want?' He strode towards her and she braced for that as best she could, but it wasn't enough. She wasn't prepared to be so close she could see the flecks of silver in his grey eyes, breathe in the scent of his alpine cologne, mingled with her spilled coffee.

'It's not that I don't love you.'

She almost choked on her breath.

'It's that I don't want you to love me. I need you to stop. Tell me you made a mistake and that you were wrong. I can't bear to think of you feeling that way about me.'

He waited, staring at her, his chest feeling as though it had been cracked in two. His eyes pleaded with her to give him what he needed. He couldn't live in a world where Beatrice loved him. The thought of disappointing her, of letting her down in some vital way, was the worst thing he could contemplate.

Hell, he'd already let her down. He could see the hurt in her face even now, days after that disastrous conversation.

She wasn't okay.

And he didn't know how to make her okay.

'There was no mistake.' She blinked at him, as though just realising something. 'And there are no regrets.' He was unprepared for her hand lightly brushing his chest, the flatness of her palm against his heart, as though she couldn't resist feeling him there. 'I'll always love you and, even though that hurts like hell right now, I'm grateful. I never thought I'd fall in love.' Her lips twisted in a poor imitation of a smile. 'I wouldn't trade the experience of falling in love with you for anything. The time we spent together was honestly the best weeks of my life.'

Her words rang with courage. He closed his eyes against it, wondering at the way the world was shifting beneath his feet, old certainties seeming to erode in the face of her determination.

'Don't you see, Ares? You're off the hook; don't beat yourself up with guilt here. You don't have to love me back. Just spending that time together was a gift.' She sniffed and he fixed his eyes on her face in time to see a single teardrop fall from the corner of one of her beautiful, expressive eyes. 'I'm not okay right now, but I will be. The pain will fade, and then I'll just have those memories. Good memories, almost all of them.'

Her heart was open to him, beautiful and forgiving, if only he'd get over his own fears and accept it. But life had made him cautious. Her heart might not have been broken, in spite of what she'd been through, but he feared his was.

And yet she was being so brave! What must it have taken Bea to face her feelings? To confide the truth of them to him. Didn't she deserve as much in return?

He ground his teeth together, his stomach unsteady as he tried to find words without overthinking them.

'I've never known anyone like you. I'd planned to fly out of London after my meeting with Clare, you know. I wasn't meant to remain here, but then I met you and you suggested I come back the next day, and I invented every excuse in the world just to see you again. You bewitched me from the start.'

Her eyes were wide but awash with disbelief. 'You were unimpressed.'

'No, I was…fascinated. Why do you think I demanded you accompany me to the ball?'

'So you wouldn't arrive alone,' she reminded him. 'So the media wouldn't get a photo of you appearing solo.'

'I go to events on my own all the time. My ego isn't so fragile, Beatrice, that I can't handle being photographed without a glamorous woman on my arm. No, it was never that.'

'So why then?' she pressed, removing her hand from his chest and curling it around her coffee cup again. She sipped it, dropping her gaze from his, pushing him away a little. He could feel that she wanted to keep him at a distance and sought to close it.

'I just wanted to be with you. I wanted to sleep with you.' He threw the words at her, needing her to understand that he was *that* kind of man. Someone who liked to seduce women he barely knew and then move on.

No mess. No emotional confusion.

'And if Cassandra hadn't quit, we would have had sex and you'd have forgotten me a week later?'

Despite what he'd thought a moment ago, he contradicted himself with a shake of his head. 'I don't think so. You were already so far under my skin, *agápi mou*. When I look back at the way I spoke to you that night, the way I threatened you—I was terrified of losing you.

I'll never forget what you said to me: that if I'd simply asked, you'd have stayed. I'd never known anyone like you before. So kind and good and compassionate. So full of love, Bea, you were aching to give it.'

Her sob was almost silent, wrenched from deep within her chest.

'You loved Danica instantly and I wanted to be a part of it.' He grimaced, the full truth of his actions spread out before him. 'Do you remember what you said, the morning you left Greece? You told me I made you fall in love with me, and you're right. Not consciously, but I was so selfish. It wasn't enough for me to have your body. I wanted all of you, everything you had to give, and that included your heart.'

She shook her head frantically. 'Don't. I can't—'

He didn't know what she was going to say, but he was getting so close to understanding his own actions. He lifted a finger to her lips, silencing her as he searched for what he'd felt and why.

'Nothing good has ever come from loving me.'

Her eyes swirled with contradictions, but she stayed quiet.

'I've loved you since that first night we met, I think, but I have no idea how to love you. I have no idea how to be a man who deserves you and, *Theós*, you deserve so much. I am being selfish again, coming here, telling you this, when the best thing for you would be if I had just let you walk away.'

Her sob was softer this time, and then she was leaning forward, pressing her forehead to his chest, her gentle sobs filling him with emotions he couldn't comprehend.

After a moment she pulled back to look up at him, shaking her head slowly. 'You're such an idiot.'

He lifted his brows.

'How do you not see yourself as you really are? How can you be so disillusioned?'

He frowned.

'You keep thinking that you let people down, but I see the opposite. I see a boy who had to parent his mother, and raise his brother. Even now, as a man in his thirties, you're picking up after Matthaios. You are good and kind and honourable, and I've got news for you, Ares.'

He waited.

'You're full of love to give as well. I watched you with Danica and saw the way you felt about her, your big, beautiful heart exploding with a need to protect her and care for her. You want to know how to be the man I deserve?'

His lips parted on a roughly expelled breath.

'By doing this! Exactly what you're doing right now. You came here today and you told me the truth about how you feel, even though that's kind of terrifying. Love isn't just an isolated emotion. It's held up by so many others! Trust and respect, kindness, humour, intention. I trust you to do the right thing by me—and that doesn't mean I'll never get hurt again. It doesn't mean you can protect me from anything bad ever happening in my life. It means that, whatever happens, I want to go through it with you.'

'But what if—'

'What if—what?' she interrupted quietly. 'Life is full of "what-ifs". The only one that matters right now is this: what if you walk out of here today and we never see each other again? Will you be able to live with *that*?'

Everything inside him froze. He stared at her, revulsion barrelling through him. 'Absolutely not.'

Her little laugh was tremulous but happy.

He groaned as realisation finally settled around his heart.

'You're right. I'm an idiot. I can't—won't—live without you. My first instinct that night was to kidnap you, take you to my home and keep you there as long as I could, and it was the right one. Please come home again, Bea. I love you.'

Her heart exploded, the word 'home' exactly what she'd been ruminating on for days. How Porto Heli had become a part of her soul without her realising it, all because of the man who lived there.

She didn't hesitate; there was no need. Bea didn't have a single doubt in her mind as to where she was meant to be, and with whom.

'I will,' she agreed, smiling up at him, her heart full. 'But not right away.' She laced their fingers together. 'I have to break it to the girls that I'm moving to Greece…'

'Oh.' He nodded. 'Then we can live here. I don't care.'

Bea laughed. 'I do. I want to come home.' The word cracked with emotion, and his expression grew serious, wondrous. 'Give me a week, okay?'

* * *

A lot changed in a week. Beatrice wasn't the only one whose life had taken an unexpected shift—Amy and Clare had revelations of their own, and excitement about their futures overlapped with frantic business meetings and staff hiring, rearranging the corporate structure to ensure the London Connection could continue to grow even with the best friends living in different cities around the world.

Of one thing they were certain: their commitment to the business—and their loyalty and love for one another—would never change, no matter how far apart they were geographically. They were friends, sisters of the heart, and always would be.

EPILOGUE

'It's a pleasure to meet you.' Matthaios smiled as he drew Bea into a warm hug, kissing her on both cheeks before releasing her. His exuberance was understandable. After several weeks in the rehab facility he was clean and sober and completely committed to living a sober life. Between them, Danica squawked, lifting her hands towards Matthaios, and at the same time the little girl burst into tears, shaking with the force of her emotions.

'Aw, she's so happy to see you.' Bea's own eyes sparkled with emotion as Matthaios clutched Danica to his chest.

He spoke in Greek, low and soft, smiling as he hugged Danica as though he'd never let her go. Ares came to stand beside Bea, his arm around her waist drawing her close so that she fitted at his side perfectly. He was warm and he was home. She was home.

'She can't stop crying,' Matthaios said anxiously, without taking his eyes off the baby's face.

'She's just a little overwhelmed,' Bea reassured him.

'She has no other way to express how she's feeling, so she cries. They're happy tears, I promise.'

He nodded, kissing Danica's head, brushing their cheeks together. 'I've missed you too, little one.' He lifted his eyes to Beatrice's face, then sideways to Ares. 'Thank you both. I promise I won't let her down again.'

'I believe you.' Ares nodded. 'But we're always here for you, any time you need us.'

Bea smiled warmly, underscoring Ares's sentiments.

Later, when Danica was settled for her afternoon nap, Matthaios held a coffee cup in his hands, staring out at the idyllic ocean view. The day was warm, the water still, so Ares was already planning an evening swim with Bea, who'd gone to get changed.

'It's serious between the two of you?'

Ares turned to his brother, nodding. 'What do you think?'

Matthaios's grin was knowing. 'I think you're besotted and I'm glad. I've never seen you like this before.'

'I've never been like this before,' he said with a lift of his shoulders. 'I love her.'

'I can see that.'

Saying it felt right—and having Matthaios's quick acceptance meant everything to Ares. 'What I said before, Matt. I'm here for you. Whatever you need.'

'I appreciate that, but I've already needed you more than enough. It's time for you to live your life without worrying about me.'

'I'm not worried,' he said truthfully. 'I'm proud. Facing your demons is hard, and you've done it twice. I think you're a superhero. But even superheroes come unstuck sometimes, and if that ever happens you know I've got your back.'

Matthaios nodded, sipping his coffee. 'I know, but this time is different. I feel different. And I'm not going to risk hurting Danica ever again. I'm not going to be like Mamá.'

Ares thought about that—their mother's repeated benders, her hangovers, her disappearance.

'I'm keen to get on with my life. Get back to work. I have to be someone Ingrid would have been proud of—I owe that to her.'

'Yes,' Ares agreed, because he finally understood what it meant to love someone with all your heart, and how that love changed you. 'You do, Matt.'

'Excuse me.' Ares turned at Ellen's interruption. Matt's eyes glanced over at the young woman. 'Bea said you wanted to be told when Danica was awake. It's her bath time.'

'And you are?' Matt prompted, standing, his manner assessing.

'This is Ellen,' Ares explained, getting to his feet. 'I told you about her.'

'I remember.' Matt extended a hand. 'Thanks for everything you've done. I appreciate it.'

'It's been my pleasure. Danica's adorable. I will be very, very sorry to see her go.'

As the two of them disappeared into the house, Ares stayed on the balcony, staring out to sea. Life was full of unexpected twists, and he could never have foreseen this. A chance meeting, an inconvenient scheduling mishap in the midst of one of the most stressful weeks of his life, had led to him finding the woman of his dreams. It was a piece of good fortune he feared he didn't deserve, but one that he knew he'd live the rest of his life being grateful for.

The sun was low in the sky but the water was still warm, lapping against Bea's sides. She clung to Ares, her legs around his waist, her arms at his neck, and she smiled because she was happy, as she'd been more often than not since coming to live with him.

Her parents had shown more than a passing interest in them as a couple, though Bea suspected that was because there was something newsworthy in her relationship with a man like Ares Lykaios, rather than being genuinely happy for her. She made a mental note to be on the lookout for pesky paparazzi, who would, no doubt, be sent by her mother, hoping for pictures to grace the pages of the tabloids. Even the thought of that couldn't dull Bea's happiness.

'They seemed so good together,' she said, thinking about Matthaios and Danica. 'He was really comfortable with her.'

'I noticed that too. I'm glad.'

'He knows he can stay with us as long as he wants, doesn't he?'

Ares nodded. 'He's keen to get back to Athens, to resume his life. His own business has been looked after by his chief financial officer, but that cannot go on for ever.'

'Let me guess. He shares your control freak gene?' she teased, kissing the tip of Ares's nose.

'I hope that's not a complaint, Beatrice Jones?'

'Absolutely not.' She blinked at him with wide-eyed innocence. 'I happen to like it when you take control.'

'I'm glad to hear it.' He emphasised his point by kicking back a little in the water, so that it was too deep for Bea to stand. She kept her legs wrapped around his waist, perfectly safe and utterly content.

'You know, when we first met, I remember you telling me that you had no intention of getting married.'

Bea tilted her head to the side, the throwaway comment one she had no recollection of making. 'Did I?'

'At the time, I paid it little attention. I thought I felt the same way.'

Her stomach lurched. 'And you don't?'

He shook his head slowly, his eyes boring into hers. 'No. Meeting you made me realise I feel the complete opposite.'

Bea's heart skipped a beat.

'I have been wondering if there's anything I might say or do to change your mind,' he said, running his hands down her back.

She sank her teeth into her lower lip, the man she loved staring at her so intently. 'To what end?'

'So that we can stand in front of our friends and family and agree to spend the rest of our lives together. What do you think?'

'Are you proposing to me?'

'Yes.' The simple response rang with determination and she laughed because she suspected he would do or say whatever it took to assure himself of her agreement. And, while her heart was already saying yes, she couldn't resist the chance to tease him a little.

'It would require a new contract,' she murmured, but her eyes showed her delight.

'Indeed.' He nodded. 'I wouldn't have expected anything less. What terms this time?'

'Hmm.' She tapped her fingers on his shoulder thoughtfully. 'Coffee in bed every morning?'

'Done. What else?'

'A lifetime of happiness?'

'And togetherness,' he tacked on.

'As little time spent with my family as possible.'

His laugh was gruff. 'Just every second Christmas.'

'Excellent. And lots of time with Danica and Matthaios.'

'And Clare and Amy.' He nodded.

She stared at him, her heart skipping a beat.

'And one day children of our own?' he suggested carefully, as though he was surprised to find himself wanting that.

Bea felt the same—it was something she'd ruled out for so long, but now she knew what she wanted, and it was more than a life with Ares. It was a life with him and a family too, children who would grow up surrounded by their love. 'Definitely.' Her voice cracked a little. 'You know, I've spent all my life feeling unwanted, and like I didn't belong anywhere.' She shook her head wistfully. 'I just didn't realise that the place I was meant to be, and the man I was meant to be with, weren't in my life yet.'

'I've been waiting for you,' he agreed quietly, 'and I didn't realise it either.'

A powerful look of understanding passed between them.

'I'm taking this as a yes,' he said as he dropped his head to hers.

'Oh, it's a yes,' she sighed, kissing him slowly. 'In fact, it's a thousand of them, and then some.'

The sunset was spectacular once again that evening, but neither of them noticed the colours in the sky. That didn't matter, though. There was a lifetime of sunsets awaiting them—every evening for the rest of their lives.

Two years later...

'You didn't have to come. I know how busy you are!' Bea fussed, reaching a hand out to Luca and Amy, smiling from ear to ear. Ares had never seen anyone so beautiful as his wife in that moment. Her face was still pink from her exertions, her hair pulled up into a loose ponytail, and all he could think was that he wanted to photograph her like this, so he could always remember her vital, incredible strength.

'As if I'd miss it,' Amy squawked.

'As if she'd let me,' Luca joked, but he showed he wasn't serious by bending down and kissing Bea's cheek before extending a hand to Ares. They shook like old friends—appropriate, given that they'd become very good friends in the intervening years, even working together on a wind turbine plant in South Africa.

'This is for you.' Amy held out an enormous box

of Bea's favourite chocolate truffles. 'I know, they're probably the last thing you can think of right now, but later tonight you might want some spoiling.'

Tears sprang to Bea's eyes—a hazard of her current emotional state. 'Thanks, Ames. They're perfect.'

'I wanted to get the bear,' Luca said with mock disappointment.

Amy rolled her expressive eyes. '"The bear" is a six-foot-tall bright blue teddy bear that would take up half of this room. Trust me, take the chocolate.'

'Oh…erm… I think we've got all the bears we need,' Bea said with a crinkled nose.

'Where is he? Where's my godson?' Clare swept into the room, all fabulous glossy brown hair and glittering blue eyes.

'*Our* godson,' Amy corrected, hugging Clare tight. Dev entered a step behind Clare.

'He's over here,' Ares said, turning to the little bundle who was sleeping, swaddled up, in a small crib to the side of Bea's bed. His heart jerked at the sight of their infant, and a love so powerful he felt as though it might swallow him burst through him.

'Lemme see, lemme see!' Clare clapped her hands together, her heels clipping across the linoleum floor. 'Oh, my goodness, he's utterly perfect, Bea. You did good, Mamá.'

Bea relaxed back against the pillows, her eyes heavy, her smile permanent.

'He is very handsome,' Dev remarked, shaking Ares's hand. 'Must get that from his mother.'

Ares laughed. 'I hope he gets just about everything

from her. If he does, then our son will be perfection itself.'

Clare and Amy shared an amused look, but Bea only had eyes for her husband.

'I ran into the twins downstairs,' Clare said, moving closer to Bea.

'Which twins?'

'Your sisters,' Clare prompted.

'Oh.' Bea's eyes skittered to Ares's. 'Mum must have told them I'd gone into labour.'

'Do you want me to ask them to come back tomorrow?' Amy asked gently.

Bea thought about that, then shook her head slowly. 'Honestly, no. They're here, and that's something I never would have thought—maybe today's a day of new beginnings,' she said with the kind of optimism that could only come from the euphoria of having given birth.

'They were just ordering coffee when we passed them, so I'd say you've got some time before they visit.'

'I'll tell them not to stay long,' Ares said, coming to place a hand on Bea's shoulder. 'You must be exhausted, and you've already had Matt here.'

'It *has* been a rather busy morning,' Bea said, but she didn't mind. Seeing Danica with her little cousin had been so heart-warming. She loved their son with all her heart, but Danica would always hold a very special place in her affections. She continued to spend as much time with her niece as possible, and knew she always would.

'On that note, we should let you have some rest,' Amy offered.

'Oh, no, please don't go,' Bea complained. 'I haven't seen you both in weeks!'

Amy nodded. 'We'll come back tomorrow.'

'And stay for lunch?'

Clare wrinkled her nose. 'Only if we can bring it. Hospital food is—'

'Totally gross,' Bea agreed. 'Deal. Dim sum?'

'Done.'

A moment later they were gone, and in the precious moments that followed, Bea allowed herself to feel completely, utterly at peace. Her heart was full and her future bright.

'I love you,' she said to her husband as her eyes drifted shut.

'And I love you.' Ares kissed her head then returned to the sleeping baby's side, his eyes trained on the infant their love had created. For so long, he'd lived in fear of being depended on by anyone, and now he could think of no greater honour than this—being needed and valued by two people as precious as his wife and child. He considered himself a very lucky man indeed.

* * * * *

HPCNMRA0521

#3917 FROM EXPOSÉ TO EXPECTING
by Andie Brock

Following one sexy night with Leonardo, journalist Emma is left mortified by his swift rejection. Letting off steam, she writes a private, scandalous exposé on the tycoon...that's accidentally *published*! Yet that's nothing compared to the surprise that follows...

#3918 THE PLAYBOY'S "I DO" DEAL
Signed, Sealed...Seduced
by Tara Pammi

Dev Kohli's superyacht is the perfect hideout from the forced marriage Clare Roberts is escaping—despite the intimacy it brings... But when the threat to her increases, so does the need to protect her with something Dev never thought he'd offer—his ring!

#3919 HIS BILLION-DOLLAR TAKEOVER TEMPTATION
The Infamous Cabrera Brothers
by Emmy Grayson

Everleigh Bradford's lost too much already to simply hand over control of the family vineyard she expected to inherit. If she must confront internationally renowned new owner Adrian Cabrera, she will! *And* fight her red-hot response to the brooding Spaniard...

#3920 QUEEN BY ROYAL APPOINTMENT
Princesses by Royal Decree
by Lucy Monroe

As a naive teenager, Lady Nataliya signed a contract promising her to a prince. Now to release them both, she causes a scandal. It works... Until her betrothed's brother, the irresistibly brooding King Nikolai, insists she honor the marriage agreement—with *him*!

YOU CAN FIND MORE INFORMATION ON UPCOMING HARLEQUIN TITLES, FREE EXCERPTS AND MORE AT HARLEQUIN.COM.

HPCNMRB0521

*Everleigh's lost too much already to simply hand over
control of the family vineyard she expected to inherit.
If she must confront internationally renowned new
owner Adrian Cabrera, she will!*

*Read on for a sneak preview of
Emmy Grayson's next story for Harlequin Presents,
His Billion-Dollar Takeover Temptation.*

"Mr. Cabrera?"

The husky feminine voice slid over his senses and sent a flash of
heat over his skin. He took another deliberate sip of his wine before
turning his attention to the second woman who had invaded his
space this evening.

Her.

His eyes drifted back up to her face in a slow, deliberate perusal.
Lush silver-blond curls enhanced her delicate features. Violet eyes
stared back at him, and her caramel-colored lips were set in a firm
line.

"Yes," he finally responded, his voice cool, showing that, despite
the unusually intense effect she was having on him, he was still in
control.

She stepped forward and held out her hand, bare except for
a simple silver band on her wrist. Adrian grasped her fingers,
pleasantly surprised by her firm grip.

"My name is Everleigh Bradford. Congratulations on your
merlot. It's exquisite."

"Thank you." He arched a brow. "While your compliments are
appreciated, was it necessary for you to ignore the balcony-closed
sign and invade my privacy?"

Everleigh's chin came up and her eyes flashed with stubborn fire.
"Yes."

HPEXP0521

Intriguing… There were plenty of men who would have cringed at the slightest hint of his disapproval. But not this woman. She stood her ground, shoulders thrown back, lips now set in a determined line.

"You're a busy man, Mr. Cabrera. I need to speak with you on an urgent matter. I'm sorry for breaking the rules, but it was necessary for me to have a moment alone with you."

Her honesty was refreshing. A night with someone as bold and beautiful as Everleigh would more than make up for his past few months of celibacy.

He infused his smile with sensuality as he raked his gaze up and down her slim form once more, this time letting his appreciation for her body show. "I would greatly enjoy a moment alone with you."

Everleigh's cheeks flushed pink. The blush caught Adrian unawares. Was she an innocent or just playing a role? Much as it would disappoint him, she wouldn't be the first to go to such lengths to catch his attention.

"This has nothing to do with sex, Mr. Cabrera."

"Adrian."

Her lips parted. "I… Excuse me?"

"Please call me Adrian."

Those beautifully shaded violet eyes narrowed. "This is a business discussion, Mr. Cabrera. First names are for friends and family."

"We could become friends, Everleigh."

What was wrong with him? He never teased a woman like this. He complimented, touched, seduced… But with this woman he just couldn't help himself.

Perhaps it was the blush. Yes, that had to be it. The delicate coloring that even now crept down her throat toward the rising slopes of her breasts…

"We will never be friends, Mr. Cabrera," Everleigh snapped. "I'm here to discuss your proposed purchase of Fox Vineyards."

"Then let's talk."